RUNAWAY

FROM THE EDGE

BOOK TWO

BY EVIE RILEY

Runaway

From The Edge

Book Two

Copyright © 2022

Evie Riley

Second Edition

ISBN: 978-1-77357-693-0

Published by Naughty Nights Press LLC

Cover Art By Willsin Rowe

RUNAWAY

Can love be enough to convince a gay homeless man to embrace that dangerous thing called hope?

Daryl Hamilton is finally free and looking forward to his new life. Coming out of the closet is the best thing he's ever done. Nothing and no one will take that freedom away from him ever again, even if it means his father is out of his life forever.

He has his art, his brother, a safe place to live, and that's really all he needs to be happy. His goals are set and he's on his way to becoming the man he's always wanted to be. A new flame in his life is just the icing on the cake.

Devon St. James left home at seventeen and has lived on the streets ever since.

He longs for the stability of a home and permanent job but doubts his crap luck will ever change. The catch twenty-two of his situation simply makes it seem impossible.

Suddenly, Devon is offered a chance at everything he desires. As usual, it's too good to last. It physically hurts to leave his new family behind but Daryl deserves a better man than him and he's determined to leave town before he hurts the only man he's ever loved.

Will Daryl's unconditional love be enough to convince Devon to stay?

Can he brave his fear and embrace the chance for a family?

Find out in the next book in the From the Edge series.

CHAPTER ONE

Daryl

THE WARM SUN against my skin felt better than it ever had before. It sounds crazy, but feeling the sun against your skin after finally becoming free, there's just something exciting in it. Exhilarating, even.

Free.

It sounds like I was in prison or

locked away in some dark and damp cellar by a serial killer. The truth is, I was just outside yesterday and every day before that. I've never been in prison. I've never been trapped in a small room and told what I could do, what I could eat. There was no serial killer causing me harm. I had every freedom that a normal human being has, and yet, I felt as if I *was* trapped. Not physically, but mentally and emotionally.

It had been almost a year since my older brother, Zane, came out to our parents. It wasn't planned. More of a heat of the moment type of deal when he was in the hospital after him and his boyfriend, Jimmy, were assaulted. They still hadn't found who had committed the brutal assault, and chances were they were never going to. They had both made peace with it, something I don't think I could have done. They were happy, though.

Zane had found a two bedroom apartment and Jimmy went off to University in Baltimore. He stays with Zane on weekends and on breaks. Currently, Jimmy was back for his four month summer vacation and, from what I have been told, they are inseparable when they aren't working.

I was proud of Zane. He was my big brother and I looked up to him a lot growing up. We have almost four years between us and when we were younger it was great. He was always teaching me something.

That four year difference, though, started to matter once he was thirteen and he didn't want to have his nine year old kid brother hanging around. We drifted apart for a while. A long while, really. It wasn't until he started working at the diner did we start to reconnect. I hadn't realized how much I had missed him until that day in our backyard.

When he came out, a flood of emotions hit me. I was slightly annoyed, because I had come out to him just months prior and he never said he was gay, too. That would have been the perfect opportunity for him to share something very personal with me.

Especially the fact that he was gay.

I was also very proud, though, because I knew what he gave up. I had made peace with the fact that I would lose my family, lose my inheritance. I was prepared for it and, to me, it wasn't worth more stress and having to deny who I was at my core.

Zane, though, he had plans. He had big plans for that money and he wasn't willing to go against our father if that meant he would lose his inheritance. When he threw it all away for love, I couldn't have been more proud of him. He made a huge sacrifice, one I knew I would be making soon enough. That sacrifice, though, became a lot less terrifying knowing I would have him in my corner.

The past ten months hadn't been easy. The exact opposite. My mother had always been indifferent with us, but now she was completely checked out. Most days, she didn't even say a word to me. It was like a zombie had taken over her body and she was just going through the motions. As for my father, well, he got worse.

Before the *incident*, as we'll call it, he was tolerable. He wasn't loving and he had never been the type of father that checked under your bed for monsters. There were no hugs, no I love yous. He was just there and you knew not to cross him. He cared about the image of his company above all else and we all knew that we had to live up to his expectations.

When you are young and innocent that is very easy to do. However, when you start to grow up and hit the teenage years, it's natural that you would want to rebel and come into your own.

We didn't do that.

The fear had already been instilled into us, even though he never raised a hand to us. My father had this unique ability to destroy you with just a few words and we knew by a single look just how much trouble we were potentially walking into.

I was twelve when I discovered that I had zero interest in girls. Changing for gym class was always hard for me. I had to make sure I kept my eyes down and didn't look at anyone for fear that my body would react. It turned out, I wasn't the only one who had that issue. Billy Swanson was fighting his own feelings of confusion and attraction.

I was thirteen when we had discovered that the other was gay as well. We had decided to create a pact with each other. A safe zone, if you will. We would get to explore our sexuality, but with each other. We shared our first kiss, first handjob, and even first blowjob, before Billy started to date a guy from another school and I was left without my safe zone.

That was, until I was sixteen and discovered Brad, my recent ex. He was deep in the closet like I was, so it seemed perfect. We had hit it off right away and within a week we were having sex.

I guess I'd always moved fast when it came to boyfriends. I don't really see the point in waiting for the right time or some special time to make a move. If I'm attracted to someone and they feel the same, then why wait? Life was short and I had zero interest in wasting any of my time on this Earth.

Brad and me didn't work out. He went and cheated on me. With a girl, no less. Since then, I'd kept to myself, trying to hide out from the hurricane that was my father. With the bomb that his oldest son, the one that was supposed to take over the company and bring it to a whole new level with marrying Kayla, was gay, he got worse.

I had no idea my father could yell so loudly and that much. He was constantly breaking things, throwing things, ranting and raving about how Zane had this *disease* and we couldn't let it infect me.

I knew I had to get out of there. I just needed to bide my time until I could graduate high school and be on my own.

Zane already had a place for me. He knew one day I would be living with him. All I needed to do was say the word.

I'd been working my ass off these past ten months to graduate early. I was now eighteen and, as of yesterday, a high school graduate. I had four months off before I would be heading for University in Baltimore.

The past ten months hadn't been easy.

Zane and me were texting and calling each other, but it'd been getting further and further apart. That wasn't on him. It was completely on me.

I'd been distancing myself from him to save him from the stress and drama of the house. He had enough on his plate, he didn't need to worry about me to go with it.

My father's words hurt, but I knew I couldn't take them personally. It was hard, because he was my father and I thought that he would love me regardless, but that just wasn't the case.

Zane had suspected it, but I'd never

confirmed that our father had been hitting me. I'd stopped counting how many bruises he had put on my body.

There wasn't one thing over another that would trigger my father to lash out at me. Sometimes, I would wear something that he felt was gay clothing. Sometimes, it was just talking about a male friend. Sometimes, it was when I was painting.

Straight men aren't artistic in my father's eyes.

It was always when he could justify my appearance or actions as that of someone *infected*. Apparently, his cure was beating it out of me. It's why I worked my ass off to graduate early. The sooner I could get out of that house, the better.

Today was that day.

I was free.

I had no home, barely any money, and no job, but I did have my car and I had Zane. Most importantly, I had my freedom. Everything else could be worked out.

I walked into the diner where I knew my brother would currently be working. I wasn't sure if Jimmy was on shift or not, but I didn't see him in the dining room. There were a few customers, but they didn't pay me any attention.

I headed behind the counter, past the kitchen, and into the back office. I knew technically I wasn't supposed to be back here, but it wasn't the first time.

I easily found Zane in the office filling out paperwork. He looked up at the sound of the door closing and I could instantly see the surprise, and then the anger, that flashed across his face.

I expected both.

The bruising from my most recent beating and the resulting black eye was still visible. It wasn't as dark as it had been a few days ago, but it was still noticeable.

"For fuck's sake, I'm going to kill him," Zane said with a deadly edge to his voice.

"Don't bother, he's not worth it." It was the first time I had admitted that the bruises had come from our father. I didn't feel one way or the other about it. It just kind of became a small piece of my history and I was determined to not let it affect me. I wasn't going to let him have power over me. "I graduated yesterday."

"What? No, your graduation is in

June," Zane said, furrowing his brows, clearly confused by what I was talking about.

"The ceremony is, but I took extra courses so I could graduate early. Officially, I'm a high school graduate as of yesterday. I packed my bag this morning, went down to have breakfast, where I told Father that I love sucking dick, and then I left. I heard the table flip over as I was shutting the door."

It was a risk telling my father that I was gay, but even if I had it to do over, it was one I would always take. I wanted him to know the reason why I was leaving. I wanted him to know that not one, but both of his sons were gay and there was nothing he could do about it. That I wasn't going to hide. I was going to make sure this whole town knew I was gay. He wasn't going to disown me and pretend that I was dead. He was going to have to deal with my face around town.

"Good for you. I'm so proud of you," Zane said, flashing me a big warm smile as he got up and pulled me in for a hug.

I easily hugged him back. I had missed how his hugs felt. He had a way of making me always feel loved and safe. After a moment, he pulled back and I spoke.

"I hope I still have that room at your place."

"It's our place and always. I have two rules, though, but they are simple and easy to follow."

"Okay," I said, slightly unsure. I wasn't really certain what type of rules Zane would have for me. Truth be told, I was hoping to live rule free.

"You go to University and get yourself a degree so you are not working in a dead end job for the rest of your life. And you need to get a part-time job to help cover your expenses. I can cover the rent, but you need to pitch in for food and to cover your car expenses."

"So, be an adult. That I can do," I said with a warm smile. I'd already planned to look for a job to help out with bills and cover my own needs. I wasn't expecting him to do that.

"Perfect. Jimmy is at his parents for dinner so he will be home late. I'll text him and let him know you'll be there. You have a key already and your room is all set up. Let me know if you need any help with University applications or figuring out a program to take."

"I've already been accepted to the University of Baltimore for the computer programming degree. I'm going to learn how to build video games. I even got a scholarship from my gaming app that I designed." I flashed him a brilliant smile, the first true smile I'd been able to let out in a very long time. I was proud of all I had accomplished, despite my father and his abuse.

I had a love of painting and drawing, but what people didn't realize was what I was doing with it. I would draw characters for video game ideas that I had floating around in my head. The work was peaceful and it allowed me to see what the characters were supposed to look like.

"I had no idea you designed a video game app. Why didn't you tell me?" Zane looked surprised, his eyebrows arched.

"I didn't think you would really care. We didn't really have the best relationship for a few years there. I just kept it to myself," I said, and shrugged.

I wasn't too sure how people would react to discovering that I was really into video games and developing them. Most teenage boys like playing video games, but to me it wasn't a hobby or a pastime. I was in love with them. I would always try to find glitches in their programming, constantly look for hidden programming in the game. They were my passion and I wanted to grow my skills and spend the rest of my life creating pieces of art.

"I know I was distant with you and I'm sorry for that. I want to know *you,* though. I want to know these things. I think it's amazing that you love playing video games and have found a way to take that love and passion and turn it into a career. That's really great, Squirt," Zane said with a warm and proud smile that reached his eyes.

I hated that nickname, but apparently it wasn't going to go away. Oh well, could be worse. Right now, I was simply happy that Zane appeared to be proud of me. That *someone* was, finally.

"I'll start looking for a job tomorrow and then I'll probably stay on campus during the week and be home on weekends."

"Yeah, that's what Jimmy does. It's not much of a drive, but it is if you are doing it twice a day. He's looking to rent a room in someone's house next year. You guys might be able to find something together."

"Yeah, I wouldn't mind that. He doing okay?"

"He's doing great," Zane said proudly, and puffed out his chest. His love for the younger man shone in his eyes whenever he talked about him, and it was very clear Zane was proud of Jimmy, too.

Jimmy had gone through a lot from the attack, including physical therapy. He never got his memories back, but I think they were taking that as a blessing.

It had taken time, but Zane seemed to have recovered from it. They had gone through something horrific together and they came out stronger than ever in the end. I couldn't have been more proud of either of them.

"That's good. All right, I'll get out of

your hair. I have to unpack and start looking for work. I'll see you tonight."

"Yes, you will. At home," Zane said, and flashed me a wink and a grin.

I couldn't help the chuckle that slipped from my lips. It sounded so weird that I was going to be living with my brother, in our own apartment. I never expected for this to ever happen, but I was looking forward to spending more time with him.

We weren't kids anymore.

We could have a real relationship. Not only between brothers, but friends, too. I really looked forward to that.

Zane and Jimmy were the only family I had left, now. We were a small family, but that never mattered to me. We all had each other and Jimmy's parents, who are amazing people.

Together, we would grow our own family and there was nothing that could stop us.

***

I arrived at the apartment and a flood of emotions hit me the moment I walked through the door.

The first, was disappointment.

Frustration in myself because I hadn't been here before.

Zane had been the one to put some distance between us growing up, but it was me that placed that wall there this time around. I had been focusing all of my energy on making it through each day, so much so that I couldn't allow myself to get close to Zane. I couldn't afford the disappointment if something were to go wrong. It was just easier to not come by whenever I was invited. Seeing the apartment for the first time shouldn't have been now and that was all on me.

I was also hit with excitement.

Anticipation of what was to come.

I had my whole future now free to do whatever I wanted with it. I was very happy about it.

The last emotion was a shockwave of anxiety that took over my body from my toes all the way up to my head. It was gone within moments, but the fact that it was there to begin with told me I hadn't exactly walked away from my father's abuse as cleanly as I thought I did.

The anxiety of him finding out where I lived, of trying to get me back, was something I would need to deal with. I had no idea if he would let me go as easily as he had Zane. I was his youngest, but also his last child that could take over the family empire.

He cared about his image and that meant if he couldn't leave his family empire to one of his sons, an empire that had been in the family for many generations, it would leave a black stain on his image. The only way to prevent that would be for him to leave it to one of his *gay* sons.

My father would never be able to leave it to a gay man, which meant he would have to try and convince one of us to go back into the closet. Considering Zane and Jimmy were not shy about kissing in public, the only one that could go back into the closet was me. I wasn't about to let that happen, but it meant I would be hearing from my father eventually and my gut was telling me it would likely be sooner rather than later.

Pushing that thought aside, I made my way through the apartment to check it all out. My room was a decent size and there was a bathroom separating mine and Zane's bedrooms. I had a feeling I was going to appreciate the added sound barrier between us.

I tossed my bag on the bed and sucked in a deep breath. I let it out slowly. This was the start of my future and I wasn't going to let anyone ruin it. Least of all, my father.

CHAPTER TWO

Devon

ST. MARKS SOUP Kitchen was one of my favorite places to be. It was not only a warm and inviting place, but the people who volunteer there were very nice. Some of the other soup kitchens and homeless shelters had some pretty judgmental volunteers.

Places like these had to take who they

could get to help out, without being paid, so they got a lot of the high school kids looking to get their community service hours in so they could graduate. Or people who were court ordered to do community service. Not the most open-minded and friendly crowd. Which was something most didn't want to deal with if they were already homeless.

I wish I could say I was here to volunteer, but I fell into the latter category. I was homeless, had been since I was seventeen and had left home. That was three years ago, now, and unfortunately, my situation hadn't improved. It wasn't for lack of trying, but when every job application asked for your address, things got a bit tricky. I'd had the odd jobs here and there, things like mowing someone's grass for twenty bucks. Sometimes, if I was lucky, I could get a laborer job for a day or two, but nothing ever stuck. It was a catch twenty-two, because I needed a place to live in order to get a proper job, but I couldn't get a place to live without a proper job. This was why the homeless community never grew smaller. We couldn't get out because we were trapped in this vicious cycle.

I made my way up to the serving area and was greeted by Roland. He was older than me. My best guess was by at least ten years. He had kind brown eyes, though, that had a way of putting you at ease, despite his rather muscular size. He was a detective for the decent size police force we had in town.

We weren't a huge town, but crime did happen and it needed to be investigated, occasionally. I had no idea what he did when he didn't have a case. In my mind, he spent his free time like some prisoner, just lifting weights all day long. The man was *huge.* I could appreciate a man that took the time to work out.

I may have been homeless, but I still enjoyed using what I had around me to stay in shape. Sometimes working out was the only thing I had to pass the time. Plus, it was free. It didn't cost anything to run through the forest or lift fallen branches. My older brother always said, keep the body strong to keep your mind sharp.

Fuck, I miss him.

"Hey, Devon, how are you doing today?" Roland asked, his New York accent poking through.

"Same as always. You?" I asked, in my terrible fake New York accent. It drove him crazy when I did it.

I had no idea what brought this man from New York over to a relatively small town in Maryland. I had never asked, afraid it was too personal. He was a detective so I had to imagine it would have been better for his career to be in a big city where there were always a hundred cases sitting on your desk.

"I'm good. You know, with the amount of times you use that terrible accent, you would think you would get better at it," Roland teased.

"I guess I'll never be an actor," I said, and let out a dramatic sigh.

Roland let out a chuckle. "You're looking better. Last time I saw you, you looked like death warmed over."

I'd felt like death had taken a hold of my body last time I was here. I had caught a really bad cold after being caught in one of Maryland's spring storms. I was soaked for a couple of days and that resulted in me getting very sick. For a bit, I was worried that I would have pneumonia. But I lucked out.

There wasn't always room at shelters. You had to get there early enough to secure a spot, and they kicked you out every morning at nine, whether you had a place to go or not. There had been plenty of times where I wasn't able to get a bed and slept rough. After three years, though, I was used to it.

"Just a bad cold. All better now."

"Anything I should know about? Any injuries I need to look over?" Roland asked, still not giving me the plate of food in his hand.

It wasn't the first time he'd had to look me over. Injuries happen when you live on the streets, but in my case especially. I was never one to look the other way like a lot of the other people do.

We had a crime rate, it wasn't astronomical, but it was there and people knew about it. The gangs were laughable, at best, but they still dealt drugs and committed violent crimes.

If someone was in trouble, I wasn't going to look the other way and pretend like I was blind and deaf. That wasn't who I was. It wasn't the type of man I was, the type of man I wanted to be. My brother would roll over in his grave if he ever saw me walk away from someone in trouble. I was not about to spit on his grave, on everything he sacrificed for me.

The end result, though, was a lot of scars from knife wounds and even a gunshot wound. Whenever I came in banged up or moving slowly, Roland always checked me over. We had an agreement between us, if I needed help I would go to him, no questions asked. If he said I needed a hospital, then we went. That was the deal and, to this day, we have both honored it.

"Nah, I'm good. With the amount of times you try and get my clothes off, people are going to think you have a thing for me," I said playfully.

I knew Roland was gay. He knew a bit about me and why I left home. We had gotten to talking one night when I had a concussion. He wouldn't let me leave for a good six hours to make sure my brain wasn't going to leak out of my ears.

It was about six months after getting to know him through St. Marks when I told him about my old man beating the hell out of me. Maybe it was the concussion that had me opening up to a virtual stranger, but that night had changed things slightly between us. We weren't really friends, but there was a shared understanding between us.

He had told me about being gay himself and how hard it was for him when he was younger. Which I had to imagine was pretty rough, considering he had ten years easily on me. Times had changed, but people wouldn't have been anywhere near as accepting of a gay man back when he was a teenager as some were now. He was a good man and had become one of my closest confidants.

"Well, as sexy as you are, you're not my type. I prefer someone smaller than you. Not to mention you're a tad hairy. I like my men clean shaven and smooth." He winked.

We were both pretty buff, and definitely had more scruff on our faces than type I went for would, and that made it perfectly clear that we would never work out. I had zero interest in a man with a hairy chest, either, and I knew Roland had that in spades.

"That is true. Looks like we have one more thing in common. We're both a sucker for a twink," I said with a smirk.

Roland laughed at that as he handed me the plate. "Be safe out there, and make sure you are checking in with me."

"Always."

We both knew that wasn't exactly true, but if something was seriously wrong I would go to him.

I took the plate and turned to face the semi large room. A quick scan had me heading over to a table closer to the back of the room where a new friend of mine was sitting.

Tyler.

We had met just a month or so ago and something had clicked instantly between us. Maybe we were kindred spirits.

Tyler and I had quite a bit in common. He had been homeless since he was eighteen, four years now. He worked odd jobs to try and earn some form of an income.

The main difference between us, though, he was straight. Even though he knew I was gay, he never cared. I think the fact that he didn't care, that he had no problem sleeping next to me, cemented our friendship.

"Hey, how are you, man?" I asked as I sat down.

Tyler gave a small shrug in response. Sometimes he got pretty quiet. I had a feeling it had to be with how he grew up. We'd never talked about it. He wasn't very chatty about his past. I had a feeling it was a rough one and I wasn't about to push or pry. I had my own rough past and I had no interest in having someone pry information out of me.

One of the larger men walked behind Tyler on his way up to the front, and Tyler instantly tensed up until the man walked by completely. Tyler had always been wary of larger men, something else I suspected was connected to his childhood.

"Have you found any work?" I asked, looking to hopefully distract Tyler and get him talking.

I wasn't sure what got him like this at times, but I knew if I asked simple questions it could get him to open up and talk. Once he was talking, he was very friendly and easy to get along with. Some days were just harder than others, which I completely understood.

"I did a painting job a week ago. You?"

"Not for a few weeks, now. I go out everyday hoping to get something. This is not how I thought my life would turn out."

And wasn't that the truth.

I know no one expects to become homeless, I sure as hell didn't. When I left at seventeen, I was only six months away from being eighteen, a legal adult. I figured it would be a short-term solution. Staying at home wasn't an option anymore. Not if I wanted to live, at least.

I figured I would bounce around on the street while still going to school. I just needed to graduate high school and then I could apply to be in the army. I wanted to be a Ranger just like my big brother, Jay. He had always been my hero. He was technically my half-brother but that changed nothing about how I felt about him.

I was only seven when he left at eighteen for the army. He made sure to call every night, though, so we could talk. He came home every chance he got leave and on holidays. There had been a few times when he came home injured, but he always said he was fine, for me to not worry about it.

He was the first person I told that I was gay when I was twelve. I was so scared of how he would react. I couldn't lose him. But, as always, he was amazing. He just told me to be careful and to always welcome love. That heartbreak would always be painful, but love was the best feeling in the world and it made the potential hurt worth the risk.

My whole world came crashing down when I was thirteen when there was a knock on the door. On the other side of it were two men in uniforms coming to deliver us a devastating blow. Jay had been killed in action while on tour.

I was devastated. I had lost my hero that day. My protector.

Things at home went downhill pretty fast after that. They were already rocky and Jay knew it.

When we were cleaning out his apartment, I found custody papers. He was going to sue our father for custody of me. Apparently, he was putting things in place so he would become an instructor and no longer in the field until I was older and could be left alone while he was on operations.

My father went from being hard to be around, to impossible. Before, he would yell, throw things, but he'd never laid a hand on me. He drank a lot, and the more he drank the more violent he got.

Jay was barely in the ground when

he hit me for the first time. I got good at lying to the people at school about where the bruises came from. We lived in a rougher area of town, so it made sense that I was having problems with gangs. I dealt with it. I pushed through, knowing that one day I would be able to leave and never have to see him again.

The very day after I graduated high school, I went down to the army recruitment office and signed up. I passed the aptitude test with flying colors. I aced the physical and everything looked like I was going to be heading out to boot camp within weeks.

I was so excited.

But it all went up in smoke when they saw my full medical file, which included the fact that I had no spleen. That instantly disqualified me for the military. Without a spleen, I was at risk of bleeding out from a non-fatal wound.

I was born with a spleen, but one night when I was fourteen my father walked in on my current boyfriend and me making out.

He lost it.

Absolutely lost it.

My boyfriend, Stan, ran out of there faster than I could blink, and he didn't look back. I broke up with him after that, I didn't need a coward in my life.

My father, though, he was uncontrollable. He beat me so badly with his fists and anything else he could get his hands on. He caused so much damage that my spleen ruptured. I almost died and the only way the doctors could save my life was by removing it.

I have to take a pill every day, now,

just so I don't bleed out. Thankfully, it was covered by government insurance when I was younger. Now, I have to get it from a free clinic, but I get a month's supply. It doesn't make you high so they have no problem giving me a month's worth at a time.

Even though I couldn't be in the military, I still figured I could get a job somewhere. I was so naive. I didn't even realize how difficult it would be to get a job without an address. The second someone discovered I was homeless there were judgments about why. They assumed I was mentally ill, or a junky. They never even bothered to ask me why.

It'd been three years, now, and I was still drowning. I needed to figure out how to swim, soon, or I would be just another statistic.

"I've been thinking about moving to a bigger city, but I'm not sure my car will be able to handle it," Tyler said.

I had been thinking the same thing. At least in a bigger city you had more opportunities to work under the table. There were more places that were willing to look the other way if it meant they could pay you a lower wage and didn't have to pay taxes for you. The trick was, I didn't have any money to afford a bus ticket. I thought about walking, but that idea really wasn't too appealing.

"I keep bouncing around with that idea, too. Larger homeless community, yes, but more opportunities for illegal workers. If I can get some money saved up, I might make the move."

"If I could just find stable work, then I

wouldn't need to move. Rent in town would be cheaper here than in Baltimore. I just need to find something," Tyler said, sounding completely frustrated.

I couldn't blame him. He had been doing this a year longer than me and I was frustrated.

I noticed that Roland kept looking over at us, but his gaze was focused on Tyler and not me. I could tell that Roland wasn't checking him out, but he still kept looking his way.

"Hey, did something happen between you and Roland?" I asked.

"Who?" Tyler asked, slightly confused.

That wasn't surprising. Tyler didn't really have a habit of talking to strangers. He kept to himself and small talk wasn't one of his strong suits.

"The big guy behind the counter in the black t-shirt, leather jacket. His name is Roland. He's a detective. He keeps looking over here at you, I didn't know if he said something to you."

"Didn't know he was a cop. And no, nothing has happened."

"He's a good guy. If you're ever in trouble and I'm not around, you can go to him. He'll help. He's gay, too, so he knows how it feels to be different and judged. He won't hit on you or anything. You don't have to worry about that. I'm just saying, he knows what it feels like to be different."

There were plenty of cops that were judgmental assholes. They saw homeless people as some sort of scum and they had zero interest in helping them or treating them like a person. Roland wasn't like that at all. He saw you as a human being who just happened to be homeless. It wasn't the first thing he saw about people, and that difference is what made me start to trust him.

"Sure," Tyler said, and I could tell he was just placating me, but I was taking it for now. "It's supposed to storm real bad tonight, do you want to crash in my car?"

This wasn't the first time Tyler had offered me a place in his car. It wasn't very comfortable, he had a small car, but we always made it work. I had noticed that the only times he offered was when it was supposed to thunderstorm. I got the feeling he was scared of storms and having me around with him helped him to feel safe. I got the impression that feeling safe wasn't something Tyler was used to. I had Jay for a while, but it seemed like Tyler didn't have anyone growing up.

"Yeah, sure, that would be great. I don't think I'll get a spot in a shelter and I don't really fancy getting soaked and sick all over again," I said, flashing him a warm smile.

I might have been able to get into a shelter for the night, but there was never a guarantee. Even if I did have a bed, I would still have agreed to Tyler's request. If me sleeping in the seat next to him helped to get him through the night, I was more than happy to do that for him. We would get through the storm together and maybe one day, we both would be able to get off the streets and make a real life for ourselves.

CHAPTER THREE

Daryl

THE PAST WEEK had been amazing. It was the first time in my life that I felt completely at ease. I didn't have to wake up to yelling. I didn't have to wake up worried about what the day was going to bring. There was no floating anxiety throughout the day. I could just be myself and be carefree.

Living with Zane was awesome. We were getting to know each other as adults and becoming more than just brothers. We were becoming friends.

He had been teaching me how to cook. We weren't very good at it, but it was fun trying out different meals and recipes. Jimmy's mother had been a wealth of knowledge that we could rely on when we got stuck. Even something like cooking dinner was fun.

We were never even allowed in the kitchen half the time growing up. So to be able to make food that we liked, instead of having to eat all this fancy shit that didn't even taste good, it was freeing. I'm sure some people would find that outrageous and weird, but whatever. Until they had lived my life, they would never truly understand how simple things are downright wonderful to me.

Another change I had enjoyed was living only ten minutes away from a park with a basketball court. I loved playing basketball. It was really the only sport I did like.

Maybe because it wasn't one my father wanted me to learn. He was always going on and on about professional quality sports that every growing businessman needed to learn. Sports like golf and fencing. Somehow they had class and things like basketball didn't. Apparently, poor degenerate people played basketball, but golf was for the upper class, those with money who could afford to be in a country club.

I never saw it that way, but because my father did it meant I couldn't be on the basketball team. That didn't stop me from playing at school and whenever I could sneak away for a few hours.

I had been going by the court every day for the past week, just shooting some hoops with the local kids that were there. I had made a few friends in the area and it felt nice to meet new people again.

Over the past week, I had noticed that there was one man in the area who would just wander through the park. He never spoke to anyone. He never joined in any of the basketball games or soccer games going on. He kept to himself, but his eyes always seemed to be scanning the park. He would watch, leaning against a tree sometimes, before he would move on.

At first, I wasn't too sure about him. I

mean, it was a man alone in a park just watching. It had a creepy factor to it. However, after getting a closer look one day, I noticed that his clothes looked old. He seemed to always be wearing roughly the same thing. Normally, a pair of old blue jeans and an older jacket. Sometimes the jacket was done up and sometimes I could see the old worn out t-shirt underneath. I knew he had more than one pair of jeans and one shirt because I had seen him wear old black jeans and a different t-shirt.

He always carried around a small black duffle bag that looked like it was about to fall apart. He had some scruff to his face, so he didn't shave every day, and some days he looked unkempt, like he hadn't showered in a few days. It was then that I figured out he wasn't watching people in a creepy way, but in an envious way. He wanted to be involved, he wanted to join in, but his obvious state of homeless was keeping him at arm's length.

It wasn't any of my business, but I couldn't help but wonder why he was homeless.

What happened to him that made him this way?

Was he on drugs?

Did he drink?

Did he lose his job and was just never able to recover?

I knew most people would automatically go with the thought of him being on drugs or a drunk, it was their natural assumption of a homeless person. I knew, though, that life was far more complicated than that. Sometimes what you see isn't always how it is.

Take my family for a perfect example.

If you saw a photo of us or saw us at one of my father's company parties, you would assume we had it all. That our lives were perfect and there was nothing that could ever stand in our way. When, in reality, that photo was fake as hell and the only time we were all smiling and together was when the photographer made us.

Everyone had a story and it was not always the story you'd expect to get out of them. Whoever he was, he had to have a story and for some reason I couldn't stop thinking about him.

I *really* couldn't stop thinking about him.

Even when I was home, I wondered where he was. On the nights when it rained, I wondered if he was somewhere warm and dry.

Was he safe?

I mean, I knew this wasn't New York City or anything, far from it, but I knew we had crimes. We had gangs that sold drugs and attacked people. Being homeless made you an easy target.

It might seem silly for me to be so worried about a complete stranger, but I had never been the type of person who walked away from someone that needed help. There was also just something about him. I don't know what, but something that made me not want to forget him.

After seven days of seeing him walking the park, I decided it was time for me to finally open my mouth.

"Hey guys, do you know who that

man is?" I asked the three guys I was playing basketball with.

"Who, Shadow?" Lucas asked with a slight nod toward the man.

"Is that his name?" I asked. That couldn't have been his real name, but I would take what I could get right now.

"Nah, we just call him that because he's always hanging around in the shadows. He never talks, never approaches anyone, just hangs around for a few hours and then leaves," Lucas said with a shrug.

"So, no one knows anything about him?" I pressed.

"We know he's been hanging around in the park for a good year, at least. Other than that, nah, man," Dave answered.

That made sense, I guess. They

wouldn't have a reason to go up to him and ask him questions. I wasn't wired that way. I wanted to know and when I had a question, I didn't stop until I got the answer. Today, I was getting some answers. At least, I hoped I would. It would really all depend on if Shadow wanted to talk to me.

After playing ball for another hour, we all started to pay up and head out. Shadow was still over by the trees, so I made my way toward him. I was pleasantly surprised when he didn't immediately start walking away. I had literally no idea if he was friendly or if he had a mental illness that would make him skeptical toward me. The last thing I wanted to do was get into a fight with someone.

"Hey, I'm new to the area. I'm Daryl,"

I said, flashing him a warm smile as I held out my hand to him.

He looked at it for a moment, slightly uncertain, as if I would pull him in to attack him or something. After a moment, he reached out and shook my hand. I was surprised to find that he had a strong grip. I don't know why I was expecting he would have a weak and shy handshake.

The second his hand touched mine, though, I noticed two things.

The first, his hands were rough, indicating he must have worked the odd job as a laborer or something equally physically demanding.

The second, and the most shocking, was when I felt a jolt of electricity go down my spine and land right in my groin. My dick pulsed for a second at the feel of his skin against mine, which was ridiculous because all he did was shake my hand. A hand I was still holding onto and really needed to let go.

"Devon," he said, as I pulled my hand back and slid it into my pocket.

His voice was a rich, deep sound that slid smoothly across my nerve endings, and it was doing nothing to calm my arousal. I couldn't help but think this man could read me the phonebook and the just the stimulating tone of his voice would have me begging for more.

"It's nice to meet you. I've seen you around for the past week as I played basketball." I nodded in the direction of the court. "I didn't know if you wanted to grab a cup of coffee or something."

It sounded like I was asking him out, but I wasn't, and I really hoped he understood that. He was attractive, though. He had dark, chocolate brown hair, and his eyes were a light caramel brown with these gold flecks in them. They were breathtaking and something I would never tire of looking at.

I could see and feel the hesitation radiating off of his body. It was almost like no one had ever asked if he wanted to grab some coffee before. That brought up more questions. Him being homeless and not getting offers for coffee made sense. But he didn't look that old, surely he couldn't have been homeless that long, so how was it he had never been asked to grab a coffee? Even with friends, it didn't have to be a girlfriend, just someone that he could hang out with.

"I'm not a prostitute," he said after a

moment, clearly figuring that was something I was after.

"Perfect, I'm not either. I would make a terrible prostitute. Not the gay part, I got that covered, but the moment they go to hand me money I would feel really awkward and probably tell them not to worry about it," I said, and flashed a grin.

I wasn't sure how he would feel about me saying I was gay, people could go either way with it. It warmed my heart, though, to see a friendly smile on his face.

"You would be a terrible prostitute," Devon easily agreed. "Coffee sounds good."

"Perfect, there's a shop just down the street."

We made our way out of the park and

we walked in silence, a comfortable quiet, which was surprising considering we had just met. I wanted to ask more questions, I had a bunch, but I also wanted to give him some time to get his own thoughts and emotions in order. I had no idea what he had been through, but I had to imagine it had been hard on him.

Once we arrived at the coffee shop, we both ordered a coffee and I ordered us each a pastry. With our order in our hands, we made our way back outside to sit on the patio to enjoy some more of the warm sun.

"Thank you for this," Devon said once we sat down.

"It's no problem. Thanks for keeping me company," I said and flashed him a warm smile.

"You didn't have anyone else to go for coffee with?" Devon challenged with a light tone.

"Honestly, no. I just moved into the area a week ago to live with my older brother and his boyfriend, who comes by on weekends. He's in Baltimore for school. I don't really know anyone in the area except for the few guys I've met playing basketball. All of my old friends from high school, I left them in my rearview."

"Why give up friends?" Devon asked, and I could tell he genuinely wanted to know.

"A week ago, I was seventeen and just about to graduate high school. I had a bunch of friends who I had basically grown up with. They all came from wealthy families like mine. They had their future mapped out for them. They were stuck up, entitled rich kids who were homophobes. So, I worked my ass off to graduate early and the day after I got my diploma, at the breakfast table, I told my homophobe parents that I was gay and moving out. I left everyone behind that would never love and accept who the real me is."

"Good for you. So many people compromise who they are just to make other people happy or to make them feel better about themselves. No one should ever have to be less than who they are just to make people more comfortable. It's better to have a handful of true friends than a hundred fake friends that you can't even be honest with. Not a lot of people understand that at your age," Devon said with a proud smile.

The fact that this complete stranger's words were making me feel all warm inside told me that there just might be more to our meeting then I thought.

A lot of people didn't believe in soulmates or fate. I don't know about soulmates, I go back and forth on the concept, but I do believe the universe has a plan for us all. That sometimes, the universe puts people in our path, people that we are supposed to meet and have in our lives for one reason or another. It would appear that Devon was one of those people that I was supposed to have in my life.

"Life is short, I have no interest in wasting any of the time. What about you? How old are you?" I wasn't sure what he was comfortable talking about so I figured it would be better to let him decide and set the pace.

"I'm twenty. No family and I have a couple of people I could call friends," Devon answered, and then paused for a moment to look at me before he continued. "You can ask, you know. I'm not going to be mad."

Ah, the elephant in the coffee shop. Well, if he was good with it, then I had no reason to make it awkward and uncomfortable.

"How long have you been homeless?" I asked gently.

"Three years, now. I left when I was seventeen. Needed to get away from my abusive father. It was either stay and potentially not see my eighteenth birthday, or leave and take my chances on the street." He shrugged.

I was shocked at how much alike we

were in that sense. I wasn't worried that my father would kill me, but the abuse was all the same.

Devon's childhood sounded like it was a pretty hard one, for at least part of it. I couldn't imagine being homeless, much less at seventeen.

I was lucky that I had Zane in my life, someone I could lean on and could count on to be there for me when times got hard.

It sounded like Devon didn't have anyone in his corner. That made for a very lonely life. A very hard and lonely life. No one should have to live that way. Life shouldn't always be a struggle. I knew everyone struggled, life wasn't perfect, people weren't perfect, but it wasn't supposed to always be a fight to see the next morning.

"Not much of a choice to make. I'm sorry you were put into that position. I was lucky in that sense. I knew I had a place to live when I left home. My older brother, Zane, he would never turn me away. When our father kicked him out for being gay, he worked as many hours as he could at a diner just so he could have a two bedroom apartment. I told him I was gay before he came out, and when he finally did, he wanted to make sure I would have a safe place to go once I was legally an adult. I don't want to think about where I might be right now if I didn't have him. I would probably be living on the streets, too."

And that was the thing, if I didn't have Zane, I wouldn't have a place to live. I know that I wouldn't have been able to live in the closet forever. I wouldn't have made it to twenty-one like Zane did. There was a very real chance I would have ended up on the street just so I wouldn't have to hide who I was.

"You're lucky to have him and it sounds like he's lucky to have you. My father discovered that I was gay when I was fourteen. He walked in on me and another kid making out. Everything pretty much went downhill after that."

I would be lying if I said there wasn't a little version of me inside doing a very happy dance. He was gay.

Holy shit, he was gay.

Maybe the universe did have a plan for me, after all, and this was fate telling me this man very well could be the one who made me believe wholeheartedly in soulmates.

"I'm sorry. My father was nothing like

yours, I'm sure, but in the past ten months there had been times where his punch landed on me. I couldn't imagine having to deal with it for years like you had to."

It had to have been terrifying for him to go through all on his own. At least, it sounded like he was all on his own.

"I'm sorry you had to go through what you did," Devon said, his eyes reflecting his understanding and the pain I'm sure his own life had cost him.

We spent the next hour just sitting there talking about little things. We kept the conversation lighter, though. I wanted to know more about him, but I didn't want it to feel like I was prying, either. We had just met and even though the conversation was easy, extremely easy, and the connection was there, we were strangers. Still, though, I didn't want the conversation to end. Mustering up some courage, I asked a question that I really hoped he answered in the affirmative.

"It's getting close to dinner time. I don't live that far from here. Do you, maybe, want to come back to my place? We can keep talking and have something to eat."

I did my best not to hold my breath as I waited for his answer. I had no idea if he would even want to keep going with our conversation or if he was looking for a polite way to leave. I really hoped it wasn't the latter option, and that he felt this connection between us as deeply as I did. I was pleasantly surprised when he didn't even take a minute to think about it.

"I would like that," Devon said, a warm smile perking the corners of his lips and reflecting in his eyes.

"Awesome," I said, with a ridiculously big smile bursting out on my face.

After tossing our garbage out, we made our way down the street toward my apartment.

"Are you sure your brother will be okay with me being there?" Devon asked, and I picked up the slight uncertainty to his voice.

"He's out with his boyfriend, Jimmy, at Jimmy's parents' place. They won't be there. But even if they were, neither of them would care," I easily said, knowing it to be true.

That was one of the best things about both Zane and Jimmy. They didn't make rash judgments on people. They were both always open-minded and understanding. Especially Jimmy. That man was a saint in another life. He also made my brother really happy and that was the only thing I cared about. I had no idea what was going to come from having Devon over for dinner, if anything, but I hoped it would at least be the start of a new friendship.

CHAPTER FOUR

Devon

WHAT THE HELL am I doing?

I don't ever grab coffee with someone I don't even know. Hell, I don't get coffee with people I *do* know, though that could be because everyone I know is homeless. When Daryl approached me, I should have turned away, I should have ignored the outstretched hand and kind eyes.

Yet, no matter how much and how hard I told myself to do just that, my body reacted on its own.

The soft skin of his hand, god, I never wanted to let it go. He was a sexy man and he had no business talking to someone like me. He was eighteen and had a lot to offer the world and someone else. I was not worth his time.

Still, he wanted to have coffee with me. He wanted to talk and know who I was. Surprisingly, he was really easy to talk with. The way the conversation flowed between us was so fluid and natural, like we were old friends just catching up. It was crazy, almost as insane as me actually going to his apartment for dinner. It's like I stepped into the twilight zone, only I never wanted to leave.

RUNAWAY

I had long since given up hope that anything good would happen to me. I knew I could never expect for someone to stand by me and help me out. If I wanted to change my life, I would have to put in the work to make it happen. I *had* been putting the work in, in fact, but it was a lot harder than I ever expected it to be.

I can't even remember the last time I had a home cooked meal. The meals at the soup kitchens were often not even hot by the time I got my plate and the taste left something to be desired, but it was food and I couldn't afford to be picky.

Growing up, a home cooked meal was whatever I could put into the microwave, and that didn't always work. One frozen dinner should not have to be microwaved for twenty minutes. Even once it was hot enough to not be frozen, it still tasted terrible. I couldn't help but wonder if Daryl could cook or not. Even if he couldn't, I was willing to bet he could make burnt toast taste good.

This could be reckless and stupid on my part. Going to a complete stranger's house was not something I did, or something I ever thought I would do. I should have told him no. I should have passed on the coffee and just walked away. That would have been the smart and safe choice to make.

Yet, here I was, walking the short distance to his apartment that he shared with two other men that could be there. Despite him saying they were at Jimmy's parents, I had no way of knowing for certain that he wasn't lying about that.

All logic dictated that I run, that I turn away right now and never look back. That would be perfectly solid logic. But here I was, still putting one foot in front of the other all the way to his apartment. I couldn't get my mind to tell my legs to turn and run. So even though it went against all reason, I followed him up the stairs, down the hallway, and into his apartment.

The apartment itself looked pretty close to what I expected for the area. It was an open concept with the exception of the island that divided the kitchen and the dining room. The walls were the stereotypical off-white color that every landlord seemed to be a fan of. There was an old wooden dining table with four chairs that were all wood, but different styles. As if they were picked up at various garage sales or second hand stores. There was an older coffee table and two end tables, a dark brown chair and sofa, and that was it for furniture. The walls, though, they caught my eye, because they all had different sized canvases on them. They were hand painted and beautiful. The artwork spoke for the room and that was clearly what made it a home.

"It's not much, but it's home," Daryl said hesitantly, mimicking my thoughts, and I could tell he was a bit self-conscious of the space. I had no idea why, especially because I lived on the streets. Anything was better than a cardboard box.

"It's great. I love the paintings," I said as I moved over to the closest one to look at it better.

"Yeah, they're great. Jimmy, he did most of them. He's going to University for art," he said proudly.

Jimmy had real talent. They were beautiful. "They're stunning. You said most of them, who did the others?"

"I did, actually," he said, his eyes downcast, cheeks pink, and a shy smile crossing his mouth.

He could paint.

I don't know why, I didn't know him well enough to know for sure, but that seemed to suit him. Looking around at all of the artwork, my gaze kept going back to the same one. It was in the living room and held some darker colors to it. It was a storm with just the slightest bit of sunlight poking through in the top right hand corner. It was my favorite out of all of them and I knew, without even having to ask, that Daryl painted it. I spoke as I moved over to it.

"This one is breathtaking. It's my favorite out of all of these pieces. You poured your heart into it."

"How did you know I painted it?" Daryl asked with the slightest bit of shock crossing his features, his eyes going wide, brows raised.

I turned to give him my full attention. Looking directly in his eyes, I spoke from the heart about the emotions running through me as a result of his painting. "I don't really know anything when it comes to art. I don't know about reading brush strokes to understand the painter's emotions at the time, or anything like that, but I do know darkness and pain. It's pretty clear in this piece that the painter was going through hard times, but was still trying to see the light through the clouds.”

It spoke to the strength that he had inside of him. He had been going through a lot, that much was clear in his words at the cafe and in this painting, however, he still tried to see the light in the world and that was inspiring.

“I painted it a month before my graduation. My parents were gone for the weekend so I broke the rules and bought painting supplies. I used to paint all the time, but after Zane came out to my parents, my father made any art forbidden in the house. He thought it was something only gay men did.”

“That’s bullshit. You have a real talent, Daryl, never give it up for anything,” I said with a deep strength to my voice as I turned to look at him. I could see he was warmed by my words. It seemed like he wasn't used to strangers complimenting his work. I had no idea why, though. He was talented, even I could see that. People should be telling him how amazing he was, how talented he was.

He headed for the kitchen as he changed the conversation. "Are you allergic to anything?"

I could tell he felt a bit self-conscious at my words, which only stirred some anger within me.

"No, I'm easy when it comes to food. What can I do to help?"

"You can sit down and keep me company," he said, flashing a warm smile.

"I can help you cook." I wasn't going to just sit there and let him do all of the work. That wasn't fair.

"You're my guest, I'm not making you cook. Seriously, sit down and relax. If you want to do something, you can talk to me. Tell me something about yourself."

I could see he wasn't going to back down on this, so I had no choice but to cave. I went and sat down on one of the stools at the island countertop.

"What would you like to know?" I was pretty much an open book. I didn't have anything to hide and I always tried to be honest with people. Didn't really see much point in lying when eventually the truth would come out.

"If you could do one job, what would it be?"

That was a loaded question. It was a simple question, something you would ask a person on a first date to get to know them. For me, though, it was not that simple. But I would answer it all the same.

"I wanted to be in the Rangers, like my older brother, Jay." That seemed to surprise him, though I wasn't sure which part.

He turned to look at me slightly as he spoke, "You have a brother?"

"I had one. He died overseas when I was thirteen." The pain from losing him was still raw and my chest hurt at just the mention of him. I forced myself to remember it wasn't a real pain and to stop myself from rubbing my chest. I wasn't really sure I would ever get over losing him. Especially like that.

"I'm so sorry, Dev. That had to be really hard. I couldn't even imagine," he said with a deep level of sympathy in his voice that told me he truly felt my pain.

"It was hard. Still is at times. He was my hero. I wanted to be just like him. So when I was twelve, I decided that I would become a Ranger and we would serve together. When I left home at seventeen, I had convinced myself that I could live on the streets until I turned eighteen and then I could enlist. I just had to make it until my eighteenth birthday. At the time, it seemed so easy to do."

Naïve.

So naive.

"What happened? I can't imagine they would turn you away if you didn't have an address. As long as you passed all of their tests, why would it matter where you were living?" he asked as he turned to work on the island counter, flattening the hamburger meat into patties.

Fuck, I love burgers.

"They were good with me being homeless, I didn't hide it from them. I passed all of their written tests with flying colors and the eye exam. I passed the physical test like it was nothing. The instructors were all impressed, said it was like I was born to be a soldier. But then the medical test came back and they discovered I had no spleen. My father had walked in on me and my secret boyfriend making out when I was fourteen. He beat me so bad, it ruptured my spleen and the only way to save my life was to remove it. I was automatically disqualified, and just like that, everything was gone."

A deeply pained look crossed his face, as if he could feel every ounce of hurt I felt at the loss of my career, my dream, my way of honoring my brother's memory. He didn't know me, I was a stranger to him, and yet, he felt empathy and concern for me. It was something I had never experienced before and I wasn't too sure how to handle it.

"I'm so sorry. The doctors never asked you what happened? Your father got away with it?"

"He did. He lied and said I had been attacked by a gang, and at the time they believed it. They had no reason to think otherwise, I guess. It wasn't like I was a frequent flyer. There were no past suspicions of abuse. I just never went to a hospital and my father was smart enough to ensure he didn't break any bones."

"Asshole. You were never able to get

back on your feet?”

"Not yet. It's hard to get a job when you don't have a set address. People assume because I'm homeless I must be a drunk or a junkie. I work out, still, use whatever I can that is lying around. That way, when I get picked up for manual labor jobs I can handle the work. I keep hoping that if I work hard enough at one of the sites they will hire me on full time, even under the table. No luck yet, though. I've been thinking about leaving town, going to a bigger one. Somewhere where there's more of a homeless population, but where they are also more open to paying someone under the table and not caring about a permanent address. I've been thinking of saving up and making the move. What about you? What's your dream?"

I was much more interested in him than talking about myself. My life was depressing enough as it was, I didn't need to drag him down with me.

"I got accepted to a University in Baltimore for video game design. I get to build my own video games. The dream would be to have my own video game company," he answered as he slid the burgers into the oven.

I couldn't stop the groan that escaped me. "God, I miss video games."

He spun around with shock and excitement plastered all over his face. "You're a gamer?"

"A very sad excuse for one. I love playing them, but I tend to be terrible at them. Unless they are the fighting or racing ones. I don't know if you'll remember this, but I used to go to the arcade that was down on Main Street."

"Crazy Ricky's Arcade, right above the pizza shop, yeah, of course I remember it. I wasted so much money on those games," he said, with a big nostalgic smile crossing his features and a chuckle slipping from his lips.

God, that laugh sounded so good.

"I know, me too. My brother, Jay, he would always take me when he was on leave. He would only play Deer Hunt, though. He held the highest score for years."

"Wait, your brother was G.I Jay? Seriously? Do you have any idea how much money and time I wasted playing on that thing just to try and beat it? I literally spent one entire summer going down there and playing it for hours every single day. All of us did. We all thought Ricky put it there just so people would keep paying to play it," he said. His tone implied he was completely amazed by the information.

"Nope. Oh, man, it was all him. There's a reason he was a sniper. He could hit anything. He taught me how to shoot playing that damn game." I subconsciously rubbed my hand across my chest again as another pang of loss and pain shot through me. I pushed off the negative thought, intent on not letting the memories get to me and ruin what was already turning out to be a great evening. It'd been so long since I'd enjoyed myself like this, with conversation and food, and, hopefully, a new friend.

"That's unreal. I actually have that game. A few years ago, they made a

Nintendo game system, a new version but with all of the old arcade games built into it. I even have the guns for it. We can play later, if you want."

"Hell, yeah," I instantly said, flashing him a big smile. I hadn't played a video game since I was fifteen when the arcade closed down, taking the last of my childhood with it. I would probably be terrible, but getting to play it again sounded like the best thing in the world. I was one lucky man tonight. I was getting a burger and to play a video game. This night might not be so bad, after all.

***

"Oh come on, how are you this good at this game?" Daryl said as he tossed his hands up in the air.

I couldn't stop laughing. For the past couple of hours, we had been playing Deer Hunt and he was terrible at it. I wasn't my brother, but I was no where near as bad as Daryl was.

"How are you this terrible at it when you own it? No wonder you could never beat Jay's score," I teased.

"I don't play it much. Why do they have to make the deer look so cute and harmless? I feel like I'm shooting Bambi."

That only made me laugh more. He was too cute for words, he really was.

"Laugh it up. I'm gonna shoot you, see how you like it." Daryl pushed me playfully on my shoulder as he spoke.

I could hear the fake clicking of the gun and I easily grabbed at it and pulled. The movement caused us both to laugh as we pretended to fight with the gun. He tossed his weight my way and it was enough for me to end up falling over and lying down on the couch with him on top of me. Suddenly, the toy gun became irrelevant with the feel of Daryl's body pressed against my own.

My desire to have him only increased and he must have felt it, too. I should have been the one to pull back, but when he closed the small gap between us, I was completely powerless. The second his lips touched mine, all sense of logic left my body.

The smoothness of his lips, the taste of him, his scent, the whole thing was intoxicating.

I wrapped my hand around the back of his neck and pulled him closer to me. I opened my legs ever so slightly, just enough for him to slip his between them, causing our rigid dicks to rub against each other. The second his rock hard erection touched mine, the only thing between us the barrier of clothing, a delicious moan escaped his lips, shattering my resolve completely.

His tongue flitted against my lips, seeking permission, and I easily gave it to him. He tasted like sweet honey and I wanted more. I could feel him, stiff against me, his throbbing heat making its way through the cloth covering him, and I knew I was just as hard, my own pulsing cock straining against my jeans to be set free.

Things between us were quickly becoming heated, our hips pressed together firmly, both of us bucking and grinding against one another, and I knew if one of us didn't stop now, we would be having sex right here on his couch. As tempting as that was, I was also fully aware of the fact that I hadn't showered in a few days. This couldn't go any further, not with me like this. After a moment, I broke the kiss, panting, and pulled back.

"Mind if I borrow your shower real quick?" I looked into his glittering, lust-filled eyes and could see his mind trying to function as he tried to catch up, change course from the scorching path we'd just been on, and he did after a brief moment.

"Yeah, second door down the hallway, right hand side."

I wanted to kiss him again, but I knew if I did, I wouldn't be able to stop. I gave a nod and started to roll, forcing him to move as well and back off of me.

I grabbed my bag and headed down the hallway and into the bathroom. After locking the door, I quickly removed my shirt and I couldn't help but look in the mirror. At one point, my skin had been unmarked, smooth and clean. Today, though, the man looking back at me was a man that had been through war. Only, it wasn't actual war. Maybe if it was, the scars that littered my body would have caused a different reaction within me. They would have represented a warrior, someone who fought bravely for this country.

Instead, mine were from abuse and years on the street. It didn't matter, in my mind, that I had gotten most of them from protecting people. I had put myself in this position when I made the decision to leave home. Had I stayed, I would have been able to get a job and I could be in my own apartment right now. It was irrational and the logical part of my brain was screaming at me that it wouldn't have mattered. I would be dead if I'd stayed. It didn't make it any easier to see the scars, though. I felt disgusted as I looked at them.

This was a mistake.

Someone like Daryl would never want someone like me. The second he saw my multitude of scars, my unflattering body, he would be horrified and disgusted, too. I shouldn't have kissed him. This was all a mistake. I knew better than this. I needed to shower and then head out. The shelters would be getting fuller by the minute and if I left it any longer I would be back on the street tonight. It was time for me to get back to reality and stop living in this fantasy world that I had been in today. We lived two different lives, in entirely different worlds, and they would never mesh together. It was time to get back to the real world.

But first, I was ready to get started with a hot shower. At least I could do that before I had to face the life I'd made for myself again. It was something.

CHAPTER FIVE

Daryl

OH MY GOD, I can't believe that just happened. I kissed him. I actually kissed him. Not only that, he kissed me back.

I knew Devon said he was gay, I had no reason to doubt him, but I just never thought he would go for a nerdy artistic guy like me. I could tell through his shirt that he worked out. I was surprised, at first, but him doing what he could outside to stay in shape for labor jobs made perfect sense to me. If employers were looking for cheap labor, they were going to go with the guy that had some muscles to him over the skinny dude.

Still, though, to feel the ripples underneath my hands, to feel his very sizeable dick rubbing against mine, it felt like a dream come true.

This hadn't been my intention when I first approached him. Not even when I invited him over for dinner. He was interesting and so easy to talk to. I didn't want the conversation to end, so it made complete sense to bring him back here to chat. I was glad I did, even before the make out session started.

He seemed like a genuinely good man who'd had a hard life. I was crushed when he spoke about losing his older brother and then losing his dream to honor him by joining the Rangers. I couldn't even imagine losing an organ because my own father had beaten me that severely. Had hated me to that level. It was soul crushing. Yet, Devon still found the strength to keep going, to carry on, and still fight for his dream. He was inspiring.

It bothered me when he spoke about leaving town. I didn't want that to happen. He had no obligation or loyalty to me, but it felt like he was leaving me behind, which was insane because we had only just met today. I shouldn't feel this close to him, this strongly connected, and yet, I did. I hoped he was feeling it, too, that it wasn't just all in my head or one-sided, because that would really suck.

The sound of the locks being turned instantly had my heart plummeting to my stomach and my hard on going soft. Great, Zane and Jimmy were back already. There went the potentially amazing sex with the gorgeous man in my shower.

"Hey, you guys are back earlier than I thought you would be," I said, but in all honesty I didn't really have an idea as to what time it actually was. A quick glance at the clock told me it was almost eight.

Shit, time flies.

"It was just dinner. Did you eat?" Zane asked.

"Yeah, I made a couple of burgers. Um... Listen, I have to tell you guys something." I wasn't too sure how they would react to this. I was positive that

Jimmy would react better than Zane.

Jimmy was the easy going one in their relationship. Don't get me wrong, I love my brother, but he needed to relax every now and then. I knew it was hard on him, though, he worked a lot of hours to pay the majority of the rent plus his car. On top of that, he was also working on a business plan for his resort and having to meet with investors. There was a lot on his plate.

"Is everything all right? Did dad contact you?" The worry was evident in Zane's voice and I hated that I had put it there. I didn't mean to.

"No, this isn't about Dad," I quickly reassured my brother. "I brought someone over. He's a really nice guy. His name is Devon."

"Oh, do you have a boyfriend?"

Jimmy asked with a big teasing smile as he flopped down on the reclining chair.

"He's not my boyfriend, no. I just met him today. Officially, anyway. I'd seen him around the park for the past week and today I finally introduced myself to him."

"So you brought a stranger over?" Zane asked, his eyebrow arched and his tone telling me he was not too impressed with me right now.

I could understand why he might not be too happy. I'd had every intention of making sure Devon was gone before they got home, but we were having so much fun, I completely lost track of time. Now, I was going to have to explain this away very quickly and pray that Devon came out of the bathroom with clothes on.

"You can't exactly expect him to never

bring someone over. It's his home, too, baby," Jimmy said lovingly, making it clear he was in my corner, for which I felt extremely grateful right at that moment.

"We went for coffee and we had such a good time talking that I invited him over for dinner. We were playing video games and we just lost track of time. He's taking a quick shower right now."

"Why would he be in the shower if you were just playing video games?" Zane asked, confusion showing on his face. He sounded skeptical and I knew I had to be honest and get it out there before things turned odd. The last thing I needed was Zane thinking anything dishonest or underhanded had been happening.

"Because he's homeless right now," I

answered slightly awkwardly.

"You brought home a stray?" Zane instantly snapped.

"Zane Hamilton! You change your attitude right now," Jimmy said with a deadly edge to his voice.

I had never heard Jimmy get angry before, and based on the look on Zane's face, he knew he'd screwed up. I didn't take it personally. I knew Zane wasn't the judgmental type. I knew he was tired and stressed. I wasn't going to hold this against him.

"I'm sorry, I'm just... It's been a long couple of weeks," Zane admitted, his voice softening.

From what I had gathered, he was having a hard time at the diner. They were not only down a dishwasher but also a cook. Zane had been working extra shifts and double shifts just to cover everything.

Finding people willing to work in a diner was easy in a larger city, but in a small town like this, it was hard to find anyone that wasn't already working. Part-time was fine for servers, but the cook was the day cook so they couldn't be in school. He had tried to get the night cook to move to days, but he could only work at night because his wife worked during the day and they had a toddler at home. The end result, my brother was ready to explode at any moment.

"I'm sorry for dropping this on you. That wasn't my intention. I didn't expect to bring him back here, but he's a good man and we were having the best conversation, so I invited him. He's twenty and has only been homeless for three years. He's worked the odd job, but he can't get anything to stick because he doesn't have an address. He left home when he was seventeen because the physical abuse by his dad was so extreme he didn't think he would make it until he was eighteen. His dad beat him so badly when he was fourteen because he found him making out with his boyfriend, he had to get his spleen removed." I knew I had rushed out all that information in a single breath, and I hoped Devon didn't get annoyed with me telling my brother about his past, but I just felt it was important for Zane to know a bit about the stranger before he met him. He needed to know.

It was hard for me to even talk about it, truth be told. The brutality of it, the fact that his father had done something like that to him and hid it from everyone, it was heartbreaking. No child should ever have to go through that, especially by his own father's hand.

I could see the information instantly affected both Zane and Jimmy. Their attack not long after they got together was still a fresh wound with them. Especially Zane. Jimmy still doesn't remember what happened to this day, but I knew it still haunted Zane. They had never found their attackers, something I suspected would leave the mental wound open until they got justice.

"Where does he stay at night?" Zane said, after a moment.

"On the street or in a shelter, if he can get in," I answered as the bathroom door opened.

My heart went into my throat and didn't go back down until I saw Devon fully dressed. He was clearly shocked to discover that we were no longer alone.

"This is my brother, Zane, and his boyfriend, Jimmy," I supplied at the slight confusion on his face.

"Devon. It's nice to meet you both," he said with a nod, before he turned to look my way. "I really appreciate today, but I have to get going if I don't want to lose a bed."

Before I could even speak up, Zane surprised me by speaking first.

"Why don't you just spend the night here. It's getting pretty late for the shelters. I know they tend to get all booked up not long past seven. I know it's not a cot, but the couch is pretty comfy to sleep on."

Instant shock went across his face and I wasn't sure if it was because I had told them he was homeless or that Zane had offered him a place to sleep tonight. I suspected it was more of a sixty-forty split in favor of the offer. Not that I could blame him. I was shocked, too.

"That's very kind of you to offer," Devon started, but Zane cut him off.

"No thanks necessary. Besides, I kinda have an ulterior motive. If you crash here tonight, that gives me more time to try and convince you to work at the diner as a dishwasher."

"What?" Devon asked, completely shocked.

"Yeah, well, the job sucks. I'm not just saying that, either. I've been told by the last five dishwashers that I've hired within the past three months. One even told me he would rather pick up roadkill instead. It's not just washing the dishes by hand, because we can't afford a fancy machine, nor would we have anywhere to put it. But the dishwasher also has to help unload the delivery truck every week so you have to be able to lift fifty-pound bags over and over again. If you crash here tonight, that gives me some time to try and convince you why it would be a fun job to have," Zane said with a grin.

He wasn't lying, I knew that. The job as a dishwasher at the diner was brutal on your body. It was easy work in the sense that you didn't have to think too much while doing it, but it was long hours and heavy lifting. The way Zane was going about it, though, allowed

Devon to not see it as a handout, but rather doing something to help Zane.

My respect for my brother and the way he just handled this situation rose dramatically in the space of a few seconds. This idea was perfect. It'd help Devon, and Zane.

"I'm not afraid of hard work. If you are offering me a job, I would be happy to take it," Devon easily said, still looking slightly surprised but easing into a more comfortable stance.

I would imagine even if it was picking up roadkill, he would be happy to take it just to have a job. From what I had seen in him, he didn't appear to be a man that was happy to do nothing all day. He wanted to work and I got the sense that he enjoyed working, feeling like he accomplished something in the day.

"You're hired. You can start tomorrow at nine. You don't have to worry about a uniform or anything, because you will be in the back. Tomorrow morning, we can go over the paperwork and get you official."

"Thank you, I really appreciate it," Devon said as he held his hand out, a grin turning up the corners of his lips.

My brother easily grasped Devon's hand and the two shook briefly before pulling back and stepping away with almost matching looks of relief in their eyes.

I could tell Devon seemed a bit overwhelmed with it all, not that I could blame him. He went from expecting to sleep in a shelter or on the street tonight with no job, to sleeping on our couch and getting a full-time job offer. It would be a lot to process for anyone.

I was happy that Devon would be able to spend the night here tonight. It just sucked that he would be on the couch and not in my bed. But maybe now that he would be working, he might consider staying here in town, getting his own place.

I knew Zane wouldn't fire him as long as he was doing his job. He could build a life here and maybe that would mean we would get to spend more time together. Maybe the connection we felt would have a true chance to grow into something more.

At least I hoped it would.

***

It was just after seven the following morning when I crawled from my bed. It had been hard to fall asleep last night knowing that Devon was right in the living room on the couch. I couldn't stop thinking about sneaking out there and continuing our intimate time on the couch together. Or him sneaking into my room and we could have one hell of a time in my bed. Neither happened, unfortunately, but I would get to see him this morning. After a quick stop in the bathroom, I walked into the living room and my heart sank. Devon wasn't there.

"He left thirty minutes ago. Said he needed to check in on someone before he would meet me at the diner," Zane supplied from the kitchen where he was cooking at the stove.

I knew I didn't have any right to be disappointed, but I was. I really wanted to see him this morning. To wish him a good first day at work and maybe sneak a kiss in when Zane and Jimmy weren't looking.

"I appreciate you giving him a job. He's been through a lot, but I'm pretty sure he can get back on his feet if given the chance."

"He needed a job and I needed someone that would appreciate the work even though it sucks. It made good business sense. You need to be careful around him," Zane warned.

"He's not dangerous, Z," I instantly said in Devon's defense. Just because he was homeless didn't mean he would be a danger to me and I wasn't going to tolerate anyone telling me otherwise.

"I'm not saying to be careful because I believe he's dangerous. If he wanted to physically hurt you, he could have easily done it while you were alone. I'm saying you need to be careful with your heart. I know how you are. You get attached to people very quickly. You've always been like that with friends and past boyfriends. The end result is always you getting your heart broken. Devon, he could stick around, he might get an apartment and be happy to stay in town. But he is also a transient and they tend to move around, especially if they don't have any family or friends keeping them here. Devon is on his own, there's nothing here that would make him want to put down roots. I just don't want you to get hurt if he disappears, that's all, Squirt."

He was right.

I knew he was right.

I did have to be careful with my heart

this time around. I felt a connection with Devon, but we were also strangers. I wouldn't be enough for him to stay in town if he wanted to leave. It wasn't like we were in love or had been dating a long time. And with no family, he didn't have any obligation to stay here. I hoped with him working at the diner he would want to stay, put down roots, but I couldn't allow myself to be naive in thinking that he definitely wouldn't leave.

Zane was right. I needed to be cautious and protect my heart, because if Devon did leave, I would be the one left with a broken heart. And I truly wasn't sure how many more broken hearts I could handle in my life.

CHAPTER SIX

Devon

OF COURSE, IT'S raining.

Why wouldn't it be raining?

It seemed like the rainy season was never going to end this time around. It had been raining on and off for the past week, but I had lucked out and was able to be inside for it.

Tonight, not so lucky.

I had been working at the diner for the past week and, surprisingly, I loved it. Being a dishwasher wasn't hard work, but it allowed me to do something with my hands. It felt good to get up every day and go to work, almost as if I was a normal person. A functioning member of society, once again, and it felt really good.

Daryl had come by the diner a few times to see me and we'd chatted during my break. Every day, I looked forward to when I would get to see him. I often found myself looking up whenever I heard the front door open, hope in my heart. Just setting my eyes on him caused my heart to flutter and a warmth to spread throughout my body.

I couldn't get the feeling of his lips out of my mind. How it felt to have his lithe body against mine. It drove me insane, haunted my dreams every time I closed my eyes. Still, I would rather have Daryl appear in my dreams than any other memory within my mind.

I shook my head to try and get some of the water out of my hair. It was pouring out tonight and because of the time I got off from work, there weren't any spots available at one of the shelters. I also hadn't been able to find Tyler, so I couldn't sleep in his car tonight. All of that left me stuck outside during this storm.

I had managed to find an overhang on one of the shop doorways that was empty. It was large enough to cover my body and shelter me from the heavy rain overhead, but when the wind blew in the wrong direction, I got the mist blown my way. Hopefully, this wouldn't make me sick. The last thing I wanted to do is not show up for work because I was too sick.

I only made minimum wage at the diner, but considering I wasn't making anything before, I was more than happy to get ten dollars an hour for cleaning dishes. I only needed to work there for a month or two and then I would have enough money saved up to be able to afford a bus ticket, and maybe rent a room from someone in a bigger city. I could find a job working in a diner or restaurant as a busboy or dishwasher. I just needed some money saved up to do it and this job might be the answer to my prayers.

"Devon."

The unexpected sound of my name had me snapping my head up. I knew that voice. I would never forget that voice. Daryl was walking toward me with an umbrella over his head. It was nearing eleven at night. He shouldn't be out in this weather, at this time of night, especially in this area. That wasn't smart and I knew the only reason he hadn't come across a problem on his way here was because of the rain.

"Daryl, what are you doing out here? It's not safe in this area, especially at night," I chastised once he was close enough.

He bent down so we were on the same level and a small piece of my heart went out to him. Most would have just stood there and looked down at me. He actually made the effort to bend down so we were on the same level.

"I'm looking for you. It's really bad

out tonight and it's supposed to get worse. You shouldn't be out in this, either. It's not safe and you'll end up sick. Come back to my place with me."

It was sweet of him to offer, but I doubted his brother would be too pleased by that. No, he didn't give me any grief about being there last time, but that wasn't late at night. He'd offered me a job and the last thing I wanted to do was disrespect him or give him cause to fire me.

"Your brother—" I started, but Daryl cut me off.

"Him and Jimmy are already asleep. He won't care, but we can always sneak you in and then out again in the morning. Come on, Dev, it's not safe out here for you. Not with the weather like this."

I didn't have the heart to tell him that I had been out in worse, that being in the rain or other elements was second nature to me. If it had been anyone else, I don't think I would have agreed, but the worry was thick in his voice and I knew if I said no, there was a very real chance he would just stay right here with me. I couldn't allow that to happen.

"Okay."

The biggest smile spread across his face and it damn near killed me. No man should have a smile that beautiful.

It was deadly.

We both stood up and started down the street. He made sure the umbrella covered us both and with his body close to mine, warmth began to flood through me once more.

"How has work been?" he asked after

a few moments.

"Good. Your brother has been really nice and the other workers there all seem great."

"Yeah, they are a good group of people. Jimmy used to work there before he went to school. I know from Zane that they have missed him. They're a good group. Is the work okay?"

"Yeah, it's fine. I like working. I like doing things with my hands. It's nice having a steady job right now. It's been a long time since I've been able to have steady work. I really appreciate your bother giving me the job."

"He's good like that. And he said you've been doing well."

That made me feel good. I took pride in my work, regardless of what it was. I always believed that if you were going to do something, you do it right and to the best of your ability, no matter what it was. It felt good to know that Zane was pleased with my work.

"How has work been for you?"

Daryl had been working at the community center teaching art class to kids. He had landed the job roughly a week ago and he had been really enjoying it. He loved to paint and draw so being able to make money doing it was a blessing.

"It's been amazing. The kids aren't too bad at it. Some of the younger ones are pretty terrible, but they are four or five so I can't expect much. They all really love it, though, and they are willing to give anything a try. I love how creative they all are. The things these kids think of are incredible."

"I always believed we were all born creative and then life takes that creativity away. We're all taught that it's wrong to have invisible friends: Santa Claus, the Easter Bunny, Tooth Fairy. They all become made up stories that we can't believe in anymore. Society and parents take that creativity away and kids conform to what society dictates they have to be. It's sad to think about what the world could be like if we allowed children to be as creative as they wanted."

"I completely agree. It's why I tell all of my students, regardless of their age, that they should never stop being creative and dreaming. Especially kids. They should be allowed to believe in magic and have invisible friends. Let them explore all aspects of their mind and what they are capable of."

It was nice that we could agree on that. Some people felt that kids shouldn't have their head in the clouds. But if you couldn't believe in magic and unicorns when you were younger, then when could you? It was a major part of growing up and it should be embraced.

As the wind picked up, we hastened our pace and made the rest of the journey to his apartment in a comfortable silence. Once we were inside, we made sure to be very quiet to avoid waking up Zane or Jimmy.

"You should take a shower and get warmed up. I'll meet you in my room," Daryl whispered.

I simply nodded and made my way down the hallway as quietly as possible. Once in the bathroom, I allowed myself a moment with my racing heart. I didn't think we would be sleeping in his room. I expected that I would be on the couch like last time.

My body already tingled with the prospect of being able to feel his skin against mine. He might not want anything sexual from me, though, so I would have to be careful and make sure I didn't overstep. I prayed that he did want to make out again, at least. I can't lie, I was really hoping for something more, though. I desperately wanted to feel him wrapped around me. To be inside him. My cock was already hard and throbbing just thinking about it.

I let out a slow breath to try and calm myself down. I pushed away from the door and got the shower running. I couldn't take too long in here, otherwise

I risked waking up Zane or Jimmy.

Ten minutes later, my body was both clean and warmed up. I quickly dressed in some dry clothes and made my way quietly back down the hallway to Daryl's room. I slipped inside and closed the door behind me.

Standing in Daryl's room was both nerve wracking and surreal. I couldn't stop thinking about the feel of his lithe body on top of mine when we were on his couch.

It had been a good year since I had been with someone in a sexual sense. I'd touched myself when the need became too much, but it wasn't often I found someone that I could be with. The last person I'd slept with was Jaz, a twenty-four year old prostitute that was just looking for someone to make him feel good. We'd both needed a bit of positive physical contact at the time, and when you were homeless or a prostitute, your choices were limited. That had been a year ago, though, and the itch was quickly becoming a burning sensation that was flooding my body.

Daryl was standing there, leaning against his dresser, in just a pair of black boxers and that was it. I hadn't been able to see his body fully last time, though I felt his muscles against mine. Seeing him now made my mouth water. He was even more beautiful than in my dreams.

He had well-formed muscles, but it was clear he wasn't a heavy weight lifter. He obviously worked out enough to stay in shape, but not to bulk up. His whole torso was smooth and held no hair. His skin was smooth and I couldn't see a single mark on him.

He was the complete opposite to me in that sense. His skin was unmarked and mine was covered in various scars from my father and years on the street. Despite the fact that he was standing there practically naked and I was fully clothed, he didn't seem to feel the slightest bit of shyness. He appeared fully confident in his body and his looks.

He made his way over to me and fingered the bottom of my shirt as he spoke. "You're wearing too many clothes."

I couldn't agree more, but I also knew scars were a topic where people either were bothered by them or they weren't, and I was terrified to find out if he was disgusted by them. I moved my hands down to cover his, stopping him from lifting my shirt.

"Do you not want to?" he asked gently.

I knew if I said no, then it wouldn't be an issue. We would just go to sleep. The problem wasn't that I didn't want to, I wanted it badly. I just didn't want to see disgust on his face.

"I want to, very much so. I've had a hard life, between my father and being on the streets. I'm not unmarked like you are," I admitted softly, my eyes downcast.

I hated that I felt insecure at this moment, but I couldn't help it. He had no marks on him. His skin was perfect.

"I don't care about scars. Your body is perfect to me, exactly the way you are. You don't have to hide from me, Dev."

I let out a shaky breath as he continued, raising my eyes to his and licking my lips.

"Can I take your shirt off?"

I was trying to find words to tell him that he could. But my emotions were stuck in my throat after his words to me. All I could do was nod, but thankfully that was all he needed.

Daryl grasped the bottom of my shirt and lifted the material up.

I raised my arms, letting him pull it over my head. I kept my eyes locked on his face to see what emotions would play across his features as my marked skin was revealed. I was surprised that I didn't see shock or disgust, but rather there was heat in his eyes. He somehow still found me attractive, even though my body was a roadmap of hell.

When he placed his lips against the scar on my collarbone, I couldn't help the shiver that snaked down my spine. He kissed and licked along each scar on my chest before he moved down to my stomach. His hands went to my belt. With expert fingers, he got my pants open and pushed them down as he kissed his way down my stomach.

He mesmerized me. I couldn't tear my eyes away from his face, in fear that he would either disappear or I would miss something important. He moaned at the sight of my hard dick and I knew he was very pleased by what he saw. I was not on the small side, I knew that. I had been told many times I was above average. He was clearly pleased by it and the thought sent a rush through me, my cock hardening even more.

Daryl licked his lips and then gave it a long lick from the base all the way up to my tip, groaning his appreciation.

I moaned the second the warmth of his tongue made contact with my skin.

He took my tip in his mouth and sucked, moaning at the taste of my precum on his tongue. He was so sexy like this.

I couldn't take my eyes off of him as he worked his way all the way down to my base, not an easy task. I couldn't remember the last time a man could take me all the way in his mouth. I threaded my hand through his hair, and he hummed his appreciation.

"You like that?" I asked in a husky whisper so there was no chance that anyone would hear us. I gave his hair a slight tug and Daryl moaned as a response, the vibration sending shockwaves of pleasure straight down my dick.

I could only allow him to continue for a few more minutes before I pulled his hair, forcing his mouth off me and pulling him up to me. I crushed my lips on his and instantly slipped my tongue into his mouth. As we kissed, I toed off my pants and boxers that had pooled around my ankles, then went for his, slipping the boxers down his hips to fall on the floor.

My hands tangled in his hair once more, mouth ravaging his, I moved us over to the bed. Once the back of his knees hit the edge of the mattress, I followed him down and we wiggled ourselves up the bed until his head was on the pillows, never once taking our mouths from the other.

Daryl opened his legs for me, hinting, but I knew if we started to grind against each other, I was going to come and that was not how I wanted this to go. I needed to be inside him.

Pulling back from the kiss, I spoke, "Where's your stuff?"

He reached over to the bedside table and pulled out a condom and some lube.

I wasted no time in grabbing the lube and putting some on my fingers. I kissed my way down his body until I reached his gloriously hard dick. I instantly took him all the way in my mouth, sliding down to his base. He let loose a very loud moan and I knew he was going to be a vocal partner in bed.

I loved it when my man was vocal. Moan and scream all you wanted. I loved it. The only time it wasn't a good thing was when you needed to be quiet.

Before I slipped my first finger inside of him, I moved my left hand up to his mouth and covered it. I wasn't sure if it would muffle everything, but it was better than nothing. He proved me right when I pressed my finger to his puckered hole and breached him, and he gave a deep moan at the intrusion. I was going to need to gag him at this rate.

I worked my mouth over his dick fast. I quickly added a second finger and then a third as he relaxed and pressed back against my hand. I focused on seeking out his sweet spot and I knew I hit it when he arched his back off the bed, a muffled cry escaping his lips behind my hand.

After a few more moments, I pulled

my fingers out and moved my mouth off his dick with an audible *pop.* I didn't want him to come just yet. I wanted to be in him when he did. He was getting way too close.

He gave me a delectable whine at the sudden loss of contact, but I knew he would be happy soon enough. I looked around and found exactly what I needed on the floor, a tie.

"Sit up."

"We getting freaky? I'm not saying no," he said with a sexy smirk.

I would be logging that information away for another time.

"You are loud and I love it, but your brother probably won't. We need to keep you quiet, Sweetheart," I spoke as I wrapped the tie around his mouth.

With the tie in place, I coaxed him to

lie back down before I grabbed the condom and slipped it on over my throbbing erection.

He looked so sexy with that tie in his mouth. We were both rocking on the edge and I knew this was going to be fast, but I also knew we could go around again before we got too tired.

I lined the head of my cock up with his hole and slowly pushed into his heat. I couldn't contain the moan as my mushroomed tip breached his muscles.

He pushed back against me, trying to get more of me inside of him. Taking the clue from him, I knew he was enjoying this moment just as much as I was, and I continued to push into him until I was all the way down to my base.

"Fuck, you feel so good, Sweetheart," I whispered as I rocked my hips gently, causing him to whimper.

I pulled out slowly before gently pushing back in, giving him time to adjust to my size. Once I felt him loosen up enough, I picked up my pace. I pulled out almost all the way before slamming back in, causing us both groan deeply.

I angled my hips, seeking out his sweet spot, and I knew I hit it when he all but screamed. I quickly placed my hand over his mouth once more to try and muffle his sounds. All the while, I continued to snap my hips forward and back, slamming into his tight heat, hitting his sweet spot dead on. We were both close, there was no stopping that.

I snaked my hand between us, curling my fingers around his throbbing dick, and started to jerk him off in time with my thrusts. I wanted to feel him come first. He was close and it only took a few more thrusts before he was coming hard and long. The tightening of his ass muscles and feeling his hot seed pour over my hand, pushed me over the edge. With a small growl, I came hard, pumping jet after jet of cum into the condom buried deep inside of him.

I removed my hand from his mouth, but left the tie there. Both of us panted hard as we fought to catch our breath.

Once I stopped pulsing, I gently pulled out and took the condom off, tossing it into the garbage can. Daryl went to remove the tie, but I stopped him. We weren't done yet.

"I didn't say I was done with you," I said as I bent forward and ran my tongue along his stomach, licking up his sweet juices.

"You taste so sweet, baby."

I kissed and licked my way back up to his neck as I reached over to his bedside nightstand. I moved away as I pulled out a condom and gave him a sexy smirk.

"I am nowhere near done with you, Sweetheart." I shot him a cocky grin.

A visible shiver of anticipation rippled through his body and he was already growing hard again. This night was nowhere near finished and neither of us wanted it to be.

***

Waking up with Daryl in my arms, his head against my chest, was one of the best feelings in the world. It felt remarkable that he was here with me, that we were together like this. I never expected anything like this to happen to me, especially with someone like Daryl. He was good, pure hearted, and saw the light within this world.

I used to be able to see the light, but over the years it only became dimmer and dimmer. My years being alone with my father and living on the streets had made me jaded, in a sense. Now, I generally expected for people to be bad. I didn't see the good in everyone anymore and quite often I was waiting for when they attacked me.

Daryl was the complete opposite of me. He had every reason to not approach me that day at the park a week ago. I was clearly homeless and that normally sent other people running in the opposite direction. Not Daryl, though. He walked right up to me and shook my hand, as if we were new friends meeting up. There was no hesitation, no fear inside him like there probably should have been with meeting someone like me.

Last night had been like a dream. Even if it could only happen that one time, it would be a memory and experience I would cherish forever.

A quick glance at the clock told me I had to get up and get moving. It was just before seven and I needed to get out of here before Zane or Jimmy saw me. I was torn between waking Daryl up and not. I didn't want to disturb his sleep, but I also didn't want to just sneak out on him. That wouldn't be fair to him, for him to think that last night meant nothing to me. I began to rub my hand up his back as I spoke.

"Babe."

Daryl sucked in a deep breath before he let out a soft groan. I knew he was waking up, though, so I continued to rub my hand along his back. I never wanted this moment to end, but I knew it would have to. I had to go back to reality, but at least I would always have this memory with me.

I hoped I would be able to see Daryl again and be with him, but I was also not holding my breath. Too much disappointment in my life to allow myself to truly hope. I had learned a long time ago it was better to expect the worst and never be disappointed. Sometimes, I was even surprised in a good way.

"It's too early," Daryl said, his voice groggy.

It   was   too   early,   especially considering how late it was when we finally did go to sleep. But I needed to sneak out before we got caught. I had no idea how his older brother felt about me. Yes, he gave me a job, but that didn't mean he wanted his kid brother dating some homeless guy. I really didn't want to lose my job because I had slept with Daryl.

"I know, but I gotta get going or we risk getting caught." A physical pain shot through my chest at the thought and I winced but he didn't see it, thankfully.

He sucked in another deep breath and I knew he was trying to wake up now. He slowly moved off my chest and rolled to the edge of the bed as he spoke. "Yeah, okay."

We both went through the process of

getting dressed and then slipped out of his room. I didn't hear anyone moving around so I felt a twinge of hope that we were going to make it, to get me out of the apartment before anyone even knew I'd been there.

I should have known better than to hope, though. Hope never worked out for me.

As we came to the end of the hallway, there sat Zane and Jimmy, drinking coffee in the kitchen. I hadn't even heard them get up. Apparently, I must have been more exhausted than I realized.

"Good morning," Zane said with an ever so slight edge to his voice.

I couldn't tell if he was upset with my being there or if it was because we were trying to sneak around behind his back. I had to give it to Daryl, though, he acted as if nothing was out of the norm.

"Morning. How did you guys sleep?"

"We slept good, until someone started to make a lot of muffled noises very late last night," Zane said.

I cringed internally, heat filling my cheeks. I had gagged Daryl, but he was so very vocal when it came to sex. It drove me crazy, but in a good way. It only made him more sexy, but I had wondered if we would wake someone up.

"I told him it would be Daryl, but he didn't seem to believe me," Jimmy said, flashing a big smile at Zane. There seemed to be something they weren't telling us and my money was on some sexy bet that Zane had just lost.

"I'm paying rent, I get to bring someone home if I want," Daryl said, and I picked up a slight defensive tone to his voice.

"That's not my issue at all. My issue is getting woken up by it. The last thing I want to hear is my kid brother having sex. The decent and responsible thing to do is wait until you are alone, like we do. I also don't appreciate you sneaking someone in. If you are going to do it, then don't hide it. It's not fair to the one you are trying to hide," Zane explained.

"I'm sorry we woke you. I didn't know how you would react to me bringing him home with me, and I really didn't want to make a big deal of it all. It was really nasty out last night and I just wanted to make sure Devon was okay," Daryl explained.

I stayed quiet as the conversation continued. This was between the brothers and I had no place butting in. I could understand Zane's point of view as well as Daryl's. I didn't take any of this personally, either. If I was Zane, I wouldn't be too happy that my kid brother wanted to sleep with a homeless man. It wasn't like I had a lot to offer him. I still couldn't figure out what Daryl wanted with me.

Why did he hold any interest in me?

I wasn't anything special. In fact, I was the exact opposite of special.

"It sounded like he was a lot more than okay," Jimmy quipped, a playful smirk on his mouth.

Zane closed his eyes for a moment and I could tell he was trying to mentally bleach his mind. I felt bad for him. I wouldn't want to listen to my brother having sex, either, but there was nothing I could do about it now.

"I know over the past week you have been worried about Devon, especially with it being the rainy season. I don't want you wandering around at night outside in bad areas alone and looking for him, though. We are willing to allow Devon to stay here, at least until he gets his first paycheck. Afterward, we can re-evaluate and see if there's another option for him to go where he would be safe," Zane finally said.

"Really?" Daryl asked. A huge smile turned up the corners of his mouth and made his eyes glitter in the morning light filtering in from the big glass window of the balcony door.

I gasped and shot a questioning look at Daryl, but he wasn't paying attention and didn't seem to notice. I felt shocked at what I had just heard. They were going to allow me to stay here until I got paid. This was unbelievable. No one had ever offered me a place to live. Tyler had allowed me to sleep in his car, but that was not the same thing. It wasn't for my own safety and welfare, but rather for the fact that he didn't like being alone. Zane and Jimmy were willing to open their home to me, allow me to have a place where I could sleep, in a bed, and get food. It all felt overwhelming and surreal.

"Yes. We don't want anything to happen to him, either. But there are ground rules," Zane warned.

"Very understanding ground rules," Jimmy added so we didn't think there would be any unfair expectations on either of us.

Jimmy seemed like the more fun

loving type of guy compared to Zane who appeared to be more serious. At least, from what I had discovered about him at work.

He did a great job at work and everyone who worked there all seemed to like him. He was easy to work for. As long as you did your job, he was happy with you. I had yet to hear him yell or demand anything from an employee. He was a good boss, one of the easiest ones that I'd worked for.

"He helps out like the rest of us with cooking and cleaning. And any sexual activities happen when you are alone," Zane stated. "I really don't want to wake up to those sounds at two in the morning again.

All of which were very reasonable rules and something I already planned to do.

"That's more than fair. I truly appreciate you allowing me to stay here temporarily," I said.

I didn't want to overstay my welcome, but I was relieved that I wouldn't have to be out on the street for the next week. I wasn't sure where I would be going once I did get paid, but I would at least have some money that I could use to figure it out. Maybe there was a cheap motel room I could rent out on a weekly basis.

"Thank you, Z," Daryl said with a warm smile on his delectable mouth.

"You're welcome, Squirt," Zane said, and flashed him a grin and a playful wink before he continued. "I need to shower. I have to go into work early today. Inventory."

"I'll cook breakfast," Daryl offered,

heading toward the fridge.

"I'll help you," I offered.

I wasn't much of a cook, but I could handle breakfast pretty easily. Besides, it was the least I could do after them allowing me to stay here. I had no idea what was going to happen in a week, but I was going to enjoy the time I would get to spend with Daryl while I could.

Odds were, Daryl was only interested in me because I was something forbidden. Soon enough, he would lose interest in me, but that was fine. I would at least get this time with him and it would be something that I cherished forever.

If Daryl wanted to use me for sex, I was perfectly fine with that. He had already given me more than anyone else in my life had. Because of him, I now had a real job that I could make a steady paycheck from. It was more than I'd had since I'd been living on the streets. Maybe, just maybe, I would allow myself to hope a tiny amount.

CHAPTER SEVEN

Daryl

THIS WAS PROBABLY the worst idea I'd ever had and chances were I was going to regret it. My father had been calling me every day since I left. Sometimes, I would let it go to voicemail, only to torture myself later by listening to the messages, and then sometimes I hit the decline button right away.

After almost three weeks, I thought he would have given up. I knew when Zane left home after the explosion of discovering he was gay came out, our father wanted nothing to do with him. All of Zane's photos were gone, his room was completely cleared out, and our father even went as far as hiring a cleaning company to sanitize the whole room.

He had never once tried to reach out to Zane. If he could have, our father likely would have denied even having two sons. The only thing stopping him was that it was public knowledge that my father had two sons that were active within the community.

All of the voicemails were essentially the same. He was asking me to call him back, that we needed to talk about this. I hadn't told Zane about any of it. I wasn't really sure how he would react. Our father was not a man who gave up easily and if he cast you aside, that was where you would always be.

Logically and rationally, I knew what he was doing. He wanted to try and convince me to go back into the closet or that this was simply a phase. It would be easier for him to try and convince me to not come out publicly about being gay, than to try and put the genie back in the bottle with Zane.

If my father wanted to leave the family business to one of his sons, that son would need a wife and children one day. To him, it was better for the company to force me to live a life of unhappiness just so he didn't have to leave his company in the hands of someone outside of the family. Or to leave it with one of his sons who were gay.

The irrational part of my mind, though, that emotional side, foolishly allowed me to hope that maybe, just maybe, my father wanted to meet with me so he could apologize. To express regret for all of the yelling, the bruises, the abuse that he threw my way out of his anger toward my brother. That he would see the error of his ways and want his family back, exactly the way we are.

It was foolish of me to allow myself to hope for a different outcome. It wasn't going to happen, and I knew that. Still, there was this part of me that wanted my father in my life. The part that remembered those rare moments when he was home and not working. Those exceptional moments when he would actually act like I felt a father should.

Not the times when I was so sick and he would allow me to place my head on his lap, because that never happened. And not the times he'd tucked me into bed and check for monsters under the bed, because that simply wasn't him either. But rather how, once in a while, he would give me a genuine smile when I got an A on a test or an assignment, some accomplishment that said his intelligent son lived up to the expected standards he had and he was proud of me.

My most precious memory, though, and it was one that I had never shared with anyone, not even Zane, was the one I hung onto the most and complicated the need to separate myself from my father entirely with the desire to believe even he might really care about me enough to accept me.

One day, when I was eight, father came to the school and pulled me out. At first, I thought I was in trouble, but he just smiled at me and took me to his car. He wouldn't tell me where we were going, just kept saying it was a surprise and that I would love it.

I was a ball of nerves and energy, because nothing like that had ever happened before. From as young as I could remember, I had always been told that school was important, that it was my job. I was to go to school every day and learn as much as I could, to always do my best to make my parents proud. So for my father, of all people, to take me out of school completely randomly, it was a huge deal.

I didn't know what to expect, but I didn't anticipate for my father to take me to an art museum, of all places. I had always loved drawing and painting. Zane used to tell me that I came out of our mother with a paintbrush in hand. Up until that moment, my parents had never really spoken on that matter. I always believed that to them I was just a kid being a kid.

After all, what kid doesn't draw and paint all day?

Walking into that museum only fueled my love for art. The paintings were all unbelievable and suddenly I had doubted myself.

How could I ever paint something that looked as breathtaking as the ones hanging on the walls?

How could I ever paint something that invoked all of these emotions with just a single look?

I was young, but even I understood the talent and emotions that went into every piece in that museum. There was a reason those artists had earned their place on those walls.

Father had picked up on my conflict and what he did next would never happen again. He grasped my shoulder, looked me right in the eyes, and told me to never doubt myself. That if I wanted something badly enough, I would make it happen. All I had to do was work hard and never stop believing in myself. He told me that he brought me there to show me where my art could end up one day and that he couldn't wait until he would be able to purchase a ticket to my own art viewing. It was the first and only time he had shown me any indication that he believed in me, in my art.

When I was a kid, my dream was to be an artist, but that started to change when my love of video games entered the picture. It started out as a doodle, just an idea for what a character could look like if I combined different aspects of other games. It was only a doodle, done so out of boredom sitting in my chemistry class, but that single drawing changed everything for me. It was when I discovered I could combine the two things I loved the most.

My drawings started to turn into virtual worlds filled with different possibilities. From paper, I moved to learning how to draw using a computer. There was a serious learning curve, but I had figured it out and now I planned to design video games for a living.

It was a dream come true.

As for today, I was meeting my father for coffee. He wanted to meet for lunch or dinner, but that would require me to be fully committed to the meeting. At a restaurant to share a meal, you couldn't just up and leave. If things went south, I would still be stuck there, required to share a meal with him. Coffee allowed me the freedom to get up and walk away at any point. It was a freedom that I desperately needed, because I had no idea what he was going to say to me. I wasn't doing this for him, I was doing it for me. To give me the closure that I needed. I owed it to myself to hear him out and know for one hundred percent certainty that this relationship was not repairable.

As I headed into the cafe, I easily spotted my father sitting at one of the tables in the back. I couldn't help but wonder if he chose a table in the back so we wouldn't be seen. After placing my order and grabbing my coffee, I made my way toward him.

Something that should have been normal, should have felt common, had my stomach all in knots. There was no telling why he wanted to meet so badly, why he felt the need to talk. There was no telling what he wanted to say or how it would all make me feel. I could hope for the best, but I also knew there was a higher chance I would leave here today feeling upset and hurt.

I slid into the seat across from him and took a moment to look at my father.

He was dressed in a typical suit, it wasn't often I would see him out of one. He looked just how I remembered him, a blank look on his face.

The perfect poker face.

We never could tell what he was thinking or feeling, something that added to the nerve-wracking experience.

"Father." I acknowledged him with a nod.

We used to be able to call him dad when we were younger, but things started to change with him. From the age of ten it went from dad to father.

"Daryl, thank you for taking the time to meet with me today, he said, his face stoic and impassive." His professional tone got on my nerves. I was his kid, not some client.

"This isn't a business meeting,

Father. I'm supposed to be your kid. You used to be able to talk to me like a parent, like a dad. If you can't do that right now, then I'm leaving. I'm not going to be treated like some client of yours."

Ground rules. We needed ground rules and they would be set by me. If he couldn't play by my rules, then we weren't doing this.

The slight tick in his jaw told me that he wasn't happy about what I had said, but he didn't get up and he didn't immediately argue against it. He was annoyed, but I expected him to be. He liked to be in charge, in control of every conversation, and I had just all but demanded that he refrain. He sucked in a slow, deep breath before he spoke.

"How have you been, Son?"

"I'm good. Zane is good, too. He's

been working a lot at the diner and putting together a business plan for his concept. I've been working at the community center teaching beginners art to a lot of great people."

This was about me and him, but I wasn't about to let him forget that he also had another son. He helped to make us. He didn't get to disown us when we don't fit in the perfect box that he designed for us.

"Teaching art to children, is that really what you want to do?"

The way he said it had me on edge.

First, it wasn't just children that I taught and even if it was, so what?

Why not let a child explore their creativity?

Why not teach them something that they could use later on in life either within their career or as a stress reliever?

Teaching wasn't something to be looked down upon.

"I enjoy teaching them. All of them are different ages, from five year olds to sixty year olds. It allows me to use my passion to earn a living. To share it with people who enjoy it just as much as I do. As for my career, I got accepted into a Baltimore University for video game design. I even secured a scholarship from a video game that I designed. I'll be using my love for art and video games to create works of art that can not only be enjoyed, but also to be utilized as an escape. To give people from all walks of life and age a break from reality when they need it."

"I didn't know you knew how to do

that. When did you learn how to make a video game?"

He sounded genuinely surprised and confused. To him, I was always up in my room playing a video game or drawing. He never expected for me to do something with it. Mostly because, in his opinion, I would go into the family business, regardless of if I wanted to be or not.

"I taught myself, mostly. I used some of my allowance and money that I saved up to take an online coding class. From there, I used YouTube to help me learn the rest. I started drawing on my computer to create the worlds that I wanted to explore myself, with characters that I wished existed. Now, I get to learn more about it and learn new tricks and skills to start making more games. I'd like to have my own video game company. You told me once to never doubt myself, that you couldn't wait to purchase a ticket to my own art viewing. It's not a painting that can be hung on a wall, but it is a work of art that can be enjoyed and bring out emotions within someone."

"When I was fourteen, we didn't have much in the way of video games. However, we did have a few arcade games. Whenever I needed a break from reality, a break from home life and stress, I would go down to the corner arcade and I would play for hours the different games and the pinball machines. I can understand the joy and the escape that video games bring people. I stopped playing them when I was sixteen, when my Father started grooming me to take over the company." He looked thoughtful as he reminisced about his own past.

"Did you always want to take over?"

I had often wondered if this was what my father wanted for his life. To work for the family company and have all of the stress on his shoulders for it. I knew it was a stressful load he carried. That was why I never held it against him when he came home in a bad mood. Or if he had to work late and missed a birthday or holiday.

"No, it wasn't. I was a lot like you, actually. I was constantly drawing. I had sketchbooks all over the house full of drawings. Only, I drew buildings. I wanted to be an architect, but that wasn't what my father wanted for me."

That shocked me. I had never seen

him draw. Even growing up, all of the times he would come into my room or when I was at the dining room table drawing or painting, he never said anything. He never sat down and joined me. He never taught me anything he knew. It would have been the perfect opportunity for him to spend time with me.

"Why didn't you ever say anything, ever join me?"

"I gave it up a long time ago. Your grandfather was a man built on old traditional values. The business and public appearance came first. Anything outside of that didn't matter and was not allowed. Being the only child, the only son, I had to take over the business and drawing wasn't acceptable to him for a man to do. Even picking whom I would marry. I only met your mother once before we got married. That was how he was and there was no changing his mind."

"You do realize that you just described yourself, right? You tried to force Zane into a marriage so he could take over the company. A company he doesn't want to run. You disowned him, rid him of his inheritance, all because he fell in love with a man. You talk about how Grandfather was traditional and controlling, but you are doing the same thing to your sons that he did to you. Do you not see that?"

I needed him to see that. I didn't want to not have my parents in my life. I wanted to be able to go home for dinner or to just hang out with my parents, with my father. I wanted to be able to share my good news, or to talk through a problem. I wanted to bring the man that I loved over for dinner and not have to worry about knives being thrown.

Don't get me wrong, I was still pissed and hurt at his behavior toward Zane and me for the past ten or so months. Trust would have to be earned. Our relationship would have to be built from the ground up. He was in no way, shape, or form, off the hook for what he did, and if he wanted something to do with me, he would have to repair the damage he did with Zane. We were a package deal and that was something he would need to accept.

"I did not grow up in a society like you did. Being a homosexual was not openly talked about. It was something that was treated as a disease, something that needed to be kept hidden. That's not how society works for the most part now, I understand that, but I didn't expect for it to hit so close to home. I didn't handle it well when your brother came out. I was raised to be a certain way and it's ingrained deeply within me."

"Why are we here, then? I don't get it. When Zane left, you cut him off completely, erased him from the house, even had his room professionally cleaned. Yet, I leave and you won't stop calling me."

He gave a slow nod as he sucked in a breath. I knew he was trying to get his thoughts in order and for the first time, I could tell this was hard for him. He wasn't one to talk about feelings. He tended to avoid those conversations like the plague. He was going out of his comfort zone for me and I appreciated that.

"How I handled everything with Zane was wrong. My behavior in the past few months has been wrong and I apologize for that. Parents aren't supposed to have favorites, but it does happen. You have always been my favorite. I've always felt more connected to you. Perhaps it's from our love of drawing. You remind me so much of who I used to be when I was younger. I wanted you to be free to pursue your own dreams. It's why I pushed harder on Zane to take over the company. It would relieve you of that burden and you would be free to be yourself. I'm not okay with either of you being gay. I don't understand it and I don't like it. However, I don't like not seeing you more. I don't want to lose you and I know my behavior was unacceptable. I never wanted to be my father and that is exactly what happened."

"I'm not going to hide who I am, not for anyone. You don't like that I'm gay, but that isn't about to change. It's a piece of who I am and I'm not going to hide it away like I have something to be ashamed of."

I was never going to hide it again. I was out, I was proud, and the very last thing I was going to be doing was going back into that closet to be miserable.

"I'm not asking you to. I'm simply asking for you to give me a chance. It's going to take me time to accept that you are a homosexual. It's not easy for me to acknowledge it, but if I have to in order to have you in my life, then I will."

"You can't have me in your life and keep Zane dead. He's your son, too, and he doesn't deserve to be cast aside because he fell in love with a man. If you want to make things right with me, you also have to make things right with him."

I wasn't going to budge on that, either. If my father couldn't start making an effort to make it right with Zane, then he wasn't getting me. I refused to be accepted only to have my brother not be. That wasn't okay and it never would be with me.

"I know, and I will. Things between your brother and I are more complicated, but I will do my best to try and repair that relationship. I want to be in your life. I want you to be in my life and I'm sorry for everything, Son."

He sounded sincere, but I was also apprehensive about the sudden change. He had always been adamant about not accepting homosexuals. It went against everything in him, and now he was willing to try and accept it? It seemed a little too good to be true. I wanted to believe him, but I also had to be rational and safe. I couldn't put myself in the position to be hurt either physically, emotionally, or mentally. There was no trust and it would take a very long time before I could even begin to remotely trust him.

"It's going to take time. I can't trust you right now, and that trust needs to be rebuilt. I'm willing to try, but I'm apprehensive toward the sudden change. I hope you truly do mean what you say."

"I do mean it, Son. I know it will take

time, and I am more than willing to put in the time and effort to repair the damage that I've caused. All I'm asking for is a chance to make it right. With you and your brother."

"I'll give you that chance, but like I said, you have to make it right with Zane, too."

"I will. Thank you. I know it's a big ask from me."

"Time will tell if I live to regret it. Please, don't make me regret it."

This could turn out to be one of the biggest regrets that I had in my life. But it could also turn out to be the best decision I'd ever made, too. It was a toss up and the coin really could go either way on me.

Businessmen would tell you some of the best investments are the ones with the highest risks. They can cripple you, but they also have the power to give you more than you could ever hope for. My hope was that this wouldn't cripple me, but only time would tell what way the coin would land.

CHAPTER EIGHT

Devon

LETTING OUT A grunt, I lifted the heavy box of oil from the back of the delivery truck. The driver, a very overweight middle-aged man, kindly left me alone with the entire truck to unload.

Zane had told me that the job sucked and he went through quite a few dishwashers. At first, I thought he was just putting up a front so I would be able to feel like I was doing him a solid instead of me feeling like I was being given a hand out. As it turned out, I was wrong. This job really did suck.

It wasn't just washing dishes like it would be in a larger restaurant. It was on me to help unload the delivery truck and to jump in to help the cooks with whatever they needed when a rush hit and I didn't have any dishes backed up.

The thing was, I liked this job. I had done a lot of random jobs over the past few years since being homeless. Washing dishes and unloading heavy boxes didn't even come close to the worst job I'd done. I didn't work in the rain or cold weather.

I did miss the cash at the end of the day, though. It was nice to be able to have some cash in my pocket so I could get something that I needed. Right now, I was stuck having to wait for a paycheck and it was hard. I wanted to be able to contribute to the house I was currently staying in. I had been cooking and cleaning and earning my keep, but it would have been nice to help out with the bills.

The past couple of weeks had been surprisingly really good. It was the longest I had been able to stay in one place for since I left home at seventeen. I hadn't really been sure how well it would go over, at first.

Daryl and me were the very definition of new. I wasn't really sure what we were. It wasn't like what it used to be when I was younger and first started dating. People didn't ask someone to be their boyfriend once you reached my age. You had to just figure it out based on actions and the situation you were in. We were sleeping together, that was beyond amazing, but I also knew we weren't sleeping with other people.

Normally, that was a good sign, but I also knew it would be hard for either one of us to be sleeping with someone else when we were basically living together. We were trying to get to know each other on both a surface and deeper level. I was being honest with him and I could tell he was being honest with me.

As for a label for what we were, I had no idea. I would have liked to be dating him, but at the same time I would have preferred to have a more stable life before I dated someone.

I would like to have my own place,

even if it was a bachelor apartment. It would give me the privacy to be with someone. More than that, though, it would be my own place. It would be a place that would be *all* mine. It would be a safe place. The first safe place I had ever truly had. It was a huge step and it was one I desperately wanted to take.

That desire was why I was more than willing to work overtime whenever Zane needed someone. The more hours I worked, the more money I would make when I finally did get my paycheck.

The sound of the front door opening drew my eyes away from the work in front of me. I knew it was locked. I was the only one here, so anyone that entered had to have a key. I couldn't stop the smile that instantly spread across my face at the sight of Daryl walking in. He locked the door behind him and headed straight for me.

"Hey, what are you doing here?" I asked.

Daryl often came by when I was working, to share my lunch or dinner breaks with him. It was one of the best parts about working here, getting to see him every day. He had been working himself and I knew he often preferred to chill when he got home. I did as well.

We had spent many nights hanging out on the couch playing different video games or watching some television. I liked that he didn't always want to go out. He wasn't old enough to drink, but even still, most guys his age were always looking for a party to sneak into. Not Daryl. He was perfectly content to stay at home and relax.

Even if I wasn't homeless and broke, I still wouldn't go out to parties. I was more introverted in that sense. I could be polite and social, but only with the right crowd. I wasn't one for large parties, bars, or clubs. A group of friends over for dinner and a few beers, though, that sounded like a good time.

"Jimmy is back in town, so you know what they are doing," Daryl said with a smirk as he went and sat down on the counter where, typically, the dirty dishes would go.

I couldn't help but shake my head a little at that. Whenever Jimmy got home for the weekend, those two were constantly going at it. Thankfully, I worked most of the weekend so I never got to hear any of it. Daryl, though, he hadn't always been so lucky. There had been a couple of times when he came running in here because he'd walked in on them having sex very loudly.

"Well, it could be worse, they could *not* be having sex. At least the passion is still alive," I offered as I moved the last box.

"True, but a little warning couldn't hurt, either. Aren't people in the dorms supposed to leave a sock on the door or something?"

"A tie I think, actually. You could always mention it to him."

"He probably won't remember."

That was probably true. From what little I knew about Zane, he was forgetful at times. When he was at work, he always remembered everything and kept the place very organized. At the house, it was the same thing with his work for his own company. Anything that didn't fall within the two categories, though, he had a habit of forgetting.

I couldn't blame the guy. His mind was clearly busy with work and his pending company. It was natural for little things to slip and none of us held it against him. Even I could tell how hard he worked, pushed himself.

With the last box put away, I washed my hands to get rid of the dirt from the boxes before I went over to Daryl. I ran my hands up his thighs and he easily opened his legs for me to fit in between them.

"I could probably think of something fun we could do to pass the time," I said as I moved closer.

Daryl wrapped his arms around my neck and pulled me in, closing the gap between us as his lips crashed down on mine.

Being with him never got old. I had been with a few friends with benefits over the years and they tended to get boring very quickly. With Daryl, the sex was not only unbelievable, but it was also exciting no matter how many times we'd done it.

Our need rose quickly and the kiss turned heated very fast. Both of our hands were moving at a rapid pace to rid the other of their clothing. Even though we had just had sex last night, it felt like it had been months since we had seen each other.

Before my pants were removed, I grabbed my wallet and pulled out the small packet of lube and the condom that I kept there. I grabbed the edges of

Daryl's jeans and he lifted his hips enough for me to be able to pull them off, along with his boxers. I grabbed him by his hips and pulled him down closer to the edge of the counter so I would have proper access to his hole to stretch him.

"I need you." Daryl moaned the second my first finger breached him.

"I know, baby. I need you, too. But I don't want to hurt you. I'll be quick," I promised.

We were both in desperate need to feel connected to the other. It was almost as if there was a string that connected us to each other and if we let that string get too tight, we would break. I didn't believe in soulmates, not even for a second, but there was just something about Daryl that made me question that belief. I couldn't help but wonder if he felt it, too, but I was too much of a coward to voice my question.

Once Daryl felt stretched enough I pulled my fingers out of his ass and rolled on the condom. Lining my tip up with his hole, I slowly pushed myself inside of his ass.

We both moaned at the invasion. No matter how many times we'd had sex, he was still so tight, as if we were made for each other. Bit by bit, I pushed my dick inside of him until I was finally balls deep.

I held still for a moment to allow Daryl to adjust to my large size. He was already breathing heavily and I knew he wouldn't last too long. I also knew he could handle more than one round back to back, though.

I had always had a high sex drive and I could stay hard for four or five rounds before I needed a break. Most guys thought it was amazing and perfect, until they started to go for multiple rounds. I was fairly certain they thought I was bluffing or exaggerating. Most could only handle three rounds before they were the ones in need of a break.

I placed my hand in the middle of his chest and slowly pushed him down onto the counter so his back was flat against it. The counter wasn't very wide so his ass hung off, causing him to wrap his legs around my hips, which wasn't exactly what I wanted tonight. Placing my hands on his inner thighs, I pushed his legs open as wide as I could so I could watch as my dick moved in and out of his sweet hole. Pulling out almost all of the way before I pushed my dick right back inside of him, slowly, all the way down to my base. I kept my pace slow, a mixture of not wanting to hurt him and to drive him crazy. His soft moans echoed off the bare kitchen walls and I knew he was getting impatient as he tried to wiggle his hips for more friction.

"Stop teasing," he whined at me.

I couldn't help the smirk that played across my lips. "I guess we should hurry. We wouldn't want our new boss to catch us."

His deep moan told me he was more than happy to role play. "I can't lose this job. You better fuck me hard and deep."

"As you wish."

I pulled out all the way before I slammed right back in, hitting his sweet spot dead on. I was pleasantly rewarded with a deep moan. I couldn't contain my own as I watched my dick move quickly in and out of him. He was completely at my mercy, but he didn't seem the least bit bothered by it.

I continued to snap my hips hard and fast, getting as deep as humanly possible inside his tight heat. We were both a moaning mess as our need for release continued to build. I was getting close, but I wanted to feel him come first. I wanted to feel his walls close around my dick.

"Touch yourself for me, baby. I want to watch as you come."

Daryl gave me the most delicious whimper in response to my words. He moved his hand to clasp around his erection and started to jerk himself off. I knew he wouldn't last long. I could already feel his walls tightening around my dick. His dick was hard as a rock and pulsing with need, the vein on the underside visibly swollen and throbbing. It was only minutes later when he was coming hard.

"Dev!"

I watched as line after line of cum shot out of him and landed on his stomach. The added tightness of his ass pushed me over the edge with him.

"Dar," I moaned as I came hard deep inside of him.

I placed my forehead against his as we both continued to pulse, our breathing heavy. I don't know what it was about him, but our sex was always earth shattering. It was insane, but also so unbelievable I never wanted it to stop.

Maybe I was living in a fantasy world right now, but it was a world I was happy to continue to live in. At least until the bubble popped.

CHAPTER NINE

Daryl

THE DAY HAD gone by so fast I almost couldn't believe it. One second I was at work and the next thing I know, I'm looking up from my canvas and it was time to go.

The group of students that I worked with today had been amazing. The energy in the room was very positive and it really brought out the creativity in everyone. It was a great group and I was already looking forward to working with them again next week.

Devon was working tonight, so I made my way toward the diner. Over the past three weeks, since Devon had been living with me, we would often meet at the diner on his dinner break. It was a way that we could continue to get to know each other and spend more time together.

I found myself growing more and more attached to him. I knew I needed to be careful with my heart, but my heart was never a very good listener. It often fell for the wrong guys, the ones who would inevitably hurt me in the end. No matter what I did, though, my heart always seemed to go all in and it was something that was happening all over again. I had been doing my best, trying my best, to not let it happen.

There was still so much up in the air where Devon was concerned. He hadn't brought up leaving for a bigger city again, but the threat of that happening was constantly playing out in my mind. I didn't want him to leave, but I had no right to ask him to stay. He had been working for the past three weeks and he was set to get his first paycheck in a couple of days. It was also going to be a decent size one with how the pay periods went. He would be getting three weeks worth of hours on it, close to a hundred and twenty hours. It was going to be more than enough for him to go to Baltimore and potentially find a room to rent for a month. That would give him the chance to find more work and he would have an address he could use for a proper job.

He didn't have family here. There truly was nothing keeping him in our small town. It only made sense for him to spread his wings and move to a larger city. It would grant him more opportunities. I hated that I had no say in this. I hated that what we had could all come to an end and I would be the one left behind with a broken heart all over again. I knew I was doing this to myself, but that didn't take the pain away any less. I wished I could have been more like Zane. He was harder to get to know. He kept a wall up around his heart, always had. Maybe it had something to do with his relationship with our father. Or maybe he was more like our father than he thought or wanted to admit. For me, maybe it was the artist in me that made me feel things differently, more deeply than the average person.

Heading into the diner, I easily made my way around the counter and headed into the back. It wasn't unusual for me to be coming in and heading straight back. Everyone who worked here was used to it. They knew I was Zane's brother and people suspected that Devon and me were dating. Neither one of us had said we were dating. We didn't call each other boyfriends, but Devon did tend to call me pet names.

I was doing my best to not get my hopes up that those pet names meant he cared about me. I knew some guys used them just as a way of not saying the person's name. It wasn't always a term of endearment. Still, whenever he called me Babe or Sweetheart, my heart fluttered a bit.

I found him just finishing up the dishes from dinner rush. He was wearing a black t-shirt and I couldn't help but admire the view of his arms. He was the most muscular man I had ever been with and I was finding myself enjoying it.

I didn't date really skinny guys, but the guys I did tend to date weren't that muscular. They "worked out" once a week at a gym. Only, their definition of working out was using the treadmill or rowing machine. If they did lift weights they were ten pounds.

I didn't care. I was the artistic gamer guy. I had muscles, but just enough to feel confident when I took my shirt off. Devon, he had the kind of muscles that could pick me up and toss me around. I was really enjoying that level of strength.

"Hey, Babe," Devon said, flashing a warm smile in my direction.

"Hey, I brought dinner for us. Nothing fancy, just some spaghetti."

"I love spaghetti. It's my favorite."

"Worked out nicely, then," I said and flashed back a warm smile.

We had been opening up to each other for the past few weeks. Nothing too crazy and emotional, but we were learning new things about the other. There were a lot of those first date type of questions, at first. They felt awkward, though, because we had talked more in depth about our lives and growing up. It seemed weird to be asking him things like his favorite color when I knew his father had beaten him so horribly it caused him to lose his dream. Still, we were doing it so we could know each other on a surface level.

It did help to ease my nerves and fears about him leaving, just slightly, but some.

After all, who wants to get to know a person better if they were only going to leave in a month?

If he was taking the time to get to know me, he must feel something toward me and hopefully maybe he'd want to stay.

Once he finished with the dishes, we strolled out into the dinning room to sit for dinner. We were the only people out here with the dinner rush being over. The couple of servers were busy trying to get things cleaned up so they would have less to do tonight for closing.

"How was work?" Devon asked.

"It was amazing. The class that I had at the end, the energy in the room was just phenomenal. I can't wait to see 'em again next week."

"That's good. Do you paint while they are?"

"Sometimes I do, yeah. I'll paint whatever subject they are working on. It just depends on their skill level and if I need to be watching over them throughout the whole class."

"Have you been working on anything special? I know you said you were thinking up a new game to develop."

I had been mentally designing a new game that would be different to anything else out there. For starters, I was going to have it where you could choose what your character's sexuality was. For the most part, any role playing games currently out there didn't have romance involved, really, and if it did, it was always a straight guy and girl. It would appeal to the masses.

I wanted to create a game where you could choose if your character was straight, gay, bisexual, or transgender. Then the algorithm would change the game based on your choice.

So if there was a love interest and you picked gay, your love interest would switch from a woman to a man. The coding would be more intense and you would need to have serious skill to be able to keep the different scenarios functioning, but I thought it would be nice for people who are gamers, but don't fall within the traditional heterosexual category.

The other aspect of the game I wanted to create was to combine gamer favorites into one. My thought process was to have it start off in a normal, everyday realm and as the game progresses you get pulled into different portals that take you to different realms that you have to fight your way through. Like a Lord of The Rings realm, a World Of Warcraft realm, a Call of Duty realm. All of these different realms that you would have to adapt to and survive, in order to complete the quests. It would be a massive undertaking in terms of coding just to keep the different realms functioning, but the goal was it wouldn't be like anything out there.

"I've been drawing up different

sketches of what I would like the characters to look like. I also have a document going of what the quests could be and how it can all connect. It's going to be a big project and most likely will take me a few years to develop."

"Well worth it, though, if it ends up being something you are proud of. From what little you have told me, it sounds like something the gaming world would love. I would be happy to be your beta tester," he said with a grin.

Hearing that warmed my heart, because maybe it meant he might be planning to stick around. He could use his paycheck to find a room to rent for the month in someone's house here. Then he could save up enough money for his own apartment. He already had a job and Zane was very pleased with him.

He worked hard and he was always willing to put in the extra time and effort to get the job done right. He was a great worker and employee. Maybe he would stick around and we could have something real together.

My phone beeped and a quick glance told me that my father had sent me a text. Ever since our meeting, he had been reaching out to me almost every day to check in. He had switched from phone calls to text messages. Maybe he figured I was more likely to talk with him if I could just text him back. Either way, it did work. I had been messaging him back, but I also kept my guard up. I didn't send him one back right away, at first. Normally, I waited an hour or two before I would actually reply. Maybe it was me being petty, but I wanted for him to feel like I was in control of our relationship and not him. Waiting even an hour made me feel like I had the power and not him.

Some type of emotion must have flitted across my face because when Devon spoke concern laced his tone.

"Everything okay, Sweetheart?"

I hadn't told anyone about my father reaching out to me or about our meeting. Honestly, I wasn't sure how anyone would react, especially Zane and Devon. After everything that Devon went through with his own father, I didn't know what he would think of me trying to repair the relationship with mine.

As for Zane, he was protective of me and I knew he would be worried that our father would hurt me again. It was wrong to keep this a secret from Zane and I knew, eventually, it would come out. Our father would be reaching out to him soon to try and repair their relationship, too. I honestly doubted Zane was going to be willing to give our father a second chance. It was his choice and he had every right to want to keep that door closed, but I hoped that speaking with our father, even just once, would bring him closure.

"My father has been reaching out to me. He used to call every day since I left and now he texts me," I finally admitted.

It had been weighing on me keeping this secret. It shouldn't have to be a secret, but it felt like I was doing something wrong. He was my father and it should be my choice if I had a relationship with him and what type of relationship it was.

"Is he harassing you?" Devon asked, worry evident in his voice now.

"No, no. At first, he would call and I would let it go to voicemail. He just wanted to meet and talk with me about what happened. I actually met with him at a cafe for coffee about a week ago."

"You met with him? Why didn't you say anything?"

Devon was clearly worried and slightly upset. I could hear it in his voice and he had every right to be a bit upset with me. I knew what he would say. He just wanted to make sure I was safe. That even in a public place my father could have tried to hurt me. It was a valid argument and one I didn't think of at the time.

"To be honest, I wasn't sure I was even going to go, and then I figured I deserved the closure."

"I can understand that. And now he's texting you? Does that mean you are talking with him now?"

"I was expecting a lecture when I met with him. I thought he would try and convince me to go back into the closet or that I was going through a phase. He didn't. It actually went pretty well. A lot better than I ever expected it to go, honestly. He said he loved me, that he didn't understand homosexuality and it would take him time. But he did say he didn't want me to be condemned to a life of misery. He seems to be trying and he apologized for everything that happened between us. He seemed really genuine."

"That's good. Hopefully, he was being authentic. Just be careful, though. Abusers, they become nice when they think they are going to lose the person they are abusing. They tell them what they want to hear to get them back close to them, only to turn around and hurt them once more when they feel like it's safe enough to."

That had been something I had thought about as well. I believed people could change. I believed that there were people out there that would change for someone they loved. I also knew that abusers liked to be in control and have all of the power. If they felt like their partner was slipping away from them, they would change temporarily to give the other person a false hope of a better life. Only to go right back to their abusive ways when they felt like their partner was under their spell again.

I hoped my father wasn't doing that

with me. That he wasn't playing the long game and looking to get me back into the house to abuse and control me. I was being extremely cautious with him and it would stay that way until I saw real change in him. It was the best I could do, and I knew I had to give it a chance or I would regret not trying.

"I know. I'm being safe. I'm not letting myself get my hopes up or making up this big false reality of a perfect family. I haven't met him since and if I do again it will be in public. I also told him he had to make things right with Zane. I don't know what Zane will do, but that will be up to him and at least he will have the option this time around."

"Being safe is all you can do. Only time will tell how it all plays out. I hope for your sake it ends how you'd like for it to. Some relationships are repairable, I know that."

"Have you heard from your father at all since you left home?"

It was a sensitive topic and I wasn't really sure what about it was off limits or not. So far, Devon had been good with talking about it. I did make a point in letting him know if there was ever a time I asked him something that he wasn't ready to answer, or comfortable with answering, to just say so. I would understand and I would never pressure him to open up when he wasn't ready.

"No. It wasn't like what it was between you and your father. He was violent before he discovered I was gay, and with what happened afterward, there's no going back from that."

"I can understand that. I wouldn't be

able to forgive him, either. I don't know if I can even forgive my father for what he did. I do understand, though, that a lot of parents handle it the wrong way when they discover their child is gay. Especially fathers and sons. I know my father was raised in a community that didn't believe in it and it was not allowed. I actually learned that he used to draw growing up. He wanted to be an architect, but his father said he had to take over the family business as the only son. He had only met my mother once before they were married. His father set it all up. I think he was forced into being someone he's not, into living a life that he wouldn't have picked for himself. Losing his last child, I think that made him reflect back on his actions and decisions. At least, I hope that's what inspired his desire to change all of a sudden. I hope it's real and not just a manipulation tactic that he's trying."

"I hope it's real, too, Babe. There are a lot of parents that react horribly at first, but at the reality of losing their child, they see that they have to change. It'll take time for him to come around, to fully accept that you are gay. There might always be a part of him that hates it, but he won't cause you harm because of it. Give it time and take it slow. If he truly wants this to work, he will put in the effort and jump through as many hoops as you want."

I hoped he was right. That my father really did want this to work and he would be willing to follow my rules and respect my boundaries. The problem was, though, only time could truly tell.

All I could do was wait and see how it would all play out.

Tonight, though, I wasn't going to worry about anymore to do with my father. I was going to enjoy my time with Devon, for however long I would get with him.

***

I was pulled out of my drawing bubble when my phone went off. It was Zane's ringer, so I reached over and hit the answer button, putting it on speaker so I could keep drawing. Zane was at work, so I wasn't expecting any earth-shattering news.

"What's going on?" I asked, looking to cut to the chase so I could keep working on my new video game characters in peace.

"Is Devon there?"

That had me instantly stopping my hand and giving my brother my full attention. Devon was set to work the evening shift at the diner. He had gotten paid yesterday and seemed to be in good spirits. It had only been two days since we had dinner at the diner. Even though I hadn't asked him about his plans, he gave no indication that he was still intending to leave.

"No, he left for work an hour ago. He didn't show?" I asked, worried now that something could have happened to him.

"I wouldn't be calling if he did, Squirt. I know you said he had talked about leaving three weeks ago. Did he mention anything to you recently?"

"No, nothing. The way he was talking, it sounded like he was looking to stay. I never flat out asked him, though, and he never said anything. What if something happened to him?"

I was quickly reaching panic mode. Devon could have left, but he also could have gotten into trouble. He had been on the streets for years and from what little stories he had told me, he had often protected people out there. I suddenly couldn't stop thinking about all of the possibilities. All of the "what if" situations.

"I'll call Roland and have him look into it. He might know of places where Devon would go. He might not be hurt or anything, Squirt. He could have easily got caught up in something. He could have been arrested on an old warrant or something. We have no idea. Don't jump to any conclusions, okay? And stay in the apartment, in case he comes back."

"Yeah, okay. I'll wait here."

"We'll find him. I'll call Roland. I love you."

"I love you, too."

Zane hung up before I could even get my body to listen to my mind to move. Zane had told me to stay here and I knew that made sense. Still, it didn't change the fact that all I wanted to do was get out there and find him. To go and search the streets for where he might be. I hated that all I could do was sit here and wait.

There wasn't even anyone I could call who might know where he was. He had no family and he didn't seem to have any friends. All I could do was wait, once again. I was really getting tired of having to sit and wait. When Devon was found, I wasn't going to wait any longer. I was going to let him know exactly how I felt about him. Life was too short to sit around and wait.

CHAPTER TEN

Devon

STANDING IN THE bus depot was a bit surreal and heart breaking. I didn't come to this decision lightly. It had been something I had been tormenting myself with for the past week or so.

It wasn't that I didn't appreciate all of the help that Daryl and his brother Zane had given me. They had given me a job, a safe place to sleep at night, but most importantly, they had given me the freedom of no judgments. They didn't judge me. They didn't make assumptions as to who I am or what I would be like just because I was homeless. It was as if I had always been there.

It was refreshing, but terrifying, all at the same time. I hadn't really been cared for since Jay died. I'd gotten so used to being on my own and only relying on myself. Having three people, now, in my life that seemed to care about my welfare, well, it was kind of overwhelming.

I never thought I had any self-esteem issues. I knew I was homeless and that generally meant I didn't have much to offer someone, but I was confident in myself. Yes, my scars were hard, but that was on the outside. Internally, I was confident in my skills and the type of person I was. Recently, though, I felt that wavering.

I'd found myself feeling a bit self-conscious because I didn't have anything to bring to the table. I only had a job because Zane took pity on me and offered it. I only had a safe place to sleep at night because Daryl had decided we needed to be friends. They were supporting the household and I was just another freeloader. I felt like a burden and I hated that feeling.

I hated feeling like I wasn't contributing to a relationship. I hated feeling like someone needed to take care of me. I was my own man and I had always been the type in the relationship to be the strong one, to take care of my partner, and I couldn't do that with Daryl right now.

There was a huge part of me that wanted to stay here. A part that wanted me to try and find my own place and keep working at the diner until I figured out what I wanted to do for a career.

An enormous part of me wanted to be with Daryl and show him what type of man I truly was. My feelings for him were strong, stronger than any man I had ever been with. That, in and of itself, was terrifying because I wasn't used to feeling so strongly toward someone. It was almost overwhelming, even though it should be a good thing. It *was* a good thing, but it was also a new experience and with that came uncertainty.

I didn't want to hurt Daryl, but I also believed he deserved someone so much better than me. I didn't have anything to offer him. He deserved to have a man that had a good job and his own place. Someone that could make him feel secure. I might never be able to offer him that security. I might never be able to offer him the world, and he deserved to have the world.

Leaving town, leaving a place where I had a full-time job, might not seem like the smartest idea and I could agree with that. However, it wasn't just a job. It was the closeness to Daryl and his brother. I couldn't end things with Daryl and still live here, still work in the diner. I wanted to be with him, but I had to let him go. I had to let him find someone that would treat him better and give him everything he deserved.

This was breaking my heart.

I could admit to myself that I was no longer *falling* in love with him. I had fallen. That's how I knew I had to leave. I wasn't going to risk Daryl falling for me, too.

That's how I ended up at the bus depot with a one way ticket to Baltimore. It would be a big city with lots of opportunities for me. I could get a job as a dishwasher in any restaurant. Some might even pay me cash. I had enough for a ticket and to rent a room in a cheap motel for the month. I could use that as my address and hopefully find something quickly so I could continue to afford to stay at the motel. Then I'd just have to save up until I could afford first and last month's rent for a one bedroom apartment. This was the right move to make.

"Well, look who we have here, boys."

I couldn't help the internal cringe at hearing Luis' voice. I'd come outside to wait for my bus, which was set to arrive within the hour. I was on my way out of town and of course Luis had found me. Turning, I saw he wasn't alone. He had five friends with him. Of course. This was the last thing I needed.

"What do you want, Luis?" I asked, making sure my shoulders were squared and my chest puffed out. There was no way I was going to let any of them know that fear had started to edge in. One on one, I could take him. Hell, I could take three of them. But six against one were not good odds.

"Payback for Juan. You should have gotten out of town months ago, bitch."

This had been coming. I'd known it

was. We only had three gangs in town and the Draggos were one of the more violent gangs. The other two were happy to hang around on the streets and try and shake business owners down for money. The Draggos had complete control of the drugs coming and going in town and if there was a violent crime committed, you could guarantee it was one of their members. There was no reasoning with them.

I tossed my bag down as they started to circle around me. I knew this wasn't going to end well, but I would be damned if I was going to go down without one hell of a fight. One thing was for certain, come morning I was going to be very sore.

***

RUNAWAY

Beep, beep, beep, beep...

What the hell is beeping?

It needed to stop. My head was killing me. My whole body was killing me.

What the hell happened?

Beep, beep, beep, beep...

What is that?

There was only one way I was going to find out, but opening my eyes seemed like a terrible idea. It was going to hurt, I knew that much. I had no idea what happened or why I was in so much pain, but I did know that opening my eyes was going to be a decision I lived to regret. Still, I forced my eyes open. My need for answers was stronger than my need to escape the pain.

The first thing I saw was a white ceiling, followed by white walls.

A hospital.

How did I end up here?

The beeping sound was coming from my right and a quick glance down at my chest told me I had leads on it from a heart monitor. There was also that pulse or oxygen monitor thing on my right index finger. Looking down hurt my head more, but I ignored the pain for a few moments longer as I took in my appearance.

There were bruises all over my arms and my right hand was swollen and bruised. I must have been in a fight. It's the only way for it to get like that. I wore a god awful hospital gown so I couldn't see any damage done to my torso. It felt like I had a broken rib or two, though, if the pain from breathing was any indication.

Everything just hurt.

It wasn't unbearable, so I knew there was some form of pain medication going through my system. I did know, though, if it hurt this much with pain medication, I didn't want to know what it would feel like once the medication ended.

A knock at the door sent a blinding pain shooting through my skull. I had to squeeze my eyes shut just to try and stave off the increased pounding. I knew this feeling all too well. A concussion. A bad one, if the pain was any indication. Thankfully, I wasn't the type of person who threw up with a concussion. I was the type of person who needed to be left alone in a dark and quiet place until it started to heal. Not something that was easy to have living on the streets.

"Sorry," I heard Roland's soft voice

say next to me.

Forcing my eyes open once again, I took in his appearance. He wore his typical black, straight cut jeans, his black t-shirt, and black leather jacket. For a detective, he always dressed on the casual side. But I suppose in a town like this, he wouldn't need to wear suits everyday.

"What happened?" My voice was hoarse, but it didn't hurt to talk so I hadn't been strangled, at least. I counted that as a win.

"You were at the bus depot, apparently looking to leave town, I believe. Six of the Draggos found you there and they apparently wanted get revenge for you attacking Juan a couple months back when he was going to rape that girl. You fought back, but they won.

You got a concussion, three broken ribs, a bruised kidney, and your right eye is heavily bruised. It was swollen, but now it's gone down. When I got there they started to take off. I was able to grab one of the guys and we've been able to pick up the other five. They are in lockup for a few days until their bail hearing."

I was lucky I wasn't dead. When I had come across Juan in that alley with that girl, I knew what he was going to do with her. The police had been looking to take Juan off the streets for years for multiple counts of sexual assault, but none of his victims would report it or testify. He seemed to think he was untouchable and I wanted to make sure he knew he wasn't. I wanted to save that girl from a violent and traumatizing experience like that. Juan hadn't walked away unscathed. I made sure of that. I broke multiple bones, including his jaw. I knew the Draggos would be looking for retaliation, but I figured it would be after Juan healed. Apparently, I was wrong.

"I knew it was coming, I guess. I just thought I had more time. I don't remember anything after my shift at work last night."

It wasn't uncommon for people to lose their memory after sustaining a concussion. What was surprising, though, was that I had been at the bus depot. I had been toying with the idea of leaving for weeks now, but I was still on the fence. Apparently, I had jumped off that fence and had decided on leaving.

"You know that is not uncommon. You got lucky that I arrived in time. Any longer and you could have been dead."

"I guess I was lucky someone there called 911."

"No one called from there. I was already on my way to the depot to see if you were there. Zane called me when you didn't show up for your shift. You've managed to scare the living shit out of him and Daryl."

There was a lecture coming my way. It didn't matter that I was literally in a hospital bed. Roland was not going to hold any punches and I knew it. He was upset with me for leaving. Maybe because he found out I was dating Daryl or maybe because I was leaving without telling him. I knew he liked to know who was in town and who wasn't.

He was one of the few cops who actually did care about the homeless community. He liked to know if we were still in town so if we went missing he would know it wasn't because we decided to move on. I should have called him. I don't know why I wouldn't have. I must have been in a hurry or too emotional and not thinking straight. Most likely the latter.

I don't remember last night, but I knew for the past week I had been agonizing over staying or leaving. If I hadn't been with Daryl the decision would have been easy. My feelings for him had muddied the waters. I had apparently made the decision to leave.

"Why would he call you?"

I wasn't sure how much time I had lost, but it couldn't have been anywhere near the twenty-four hour mark. If Zane called to report me missing after not showing up for my shift, they wouldn't have investigated. They probably wouldn't have investigated if it had been a whole day with me being homeless. Most cops tended to assume when a homeless person went missing they had just moved on to the next town. Hoards of people didn't come together to search the area.

"Almost a year ago, Zane and Jimmy were attacked in the park. I took the case. We've gotten close since then. They were worried and asked if I wouldn't mind looking for you. I headed to the bus depot first. I figured with your new paycheck you would be running away."

"I wasn't running away," I said with as much strength to my voice that my body could muster.

"Right. That's why you are leaving not only a stable job, and a roof over your head, but also the man that you are madly in love with," Roland challenged.

"I'm not in love with him," I instantly denied. It was a lie and, based on Roland's face, we both knew it.

"Come on, Dev. who are you trying to kid here? Me or yourself? I've known you for a few years now, and the last thing you are is a coward. You don't run away. So why are you running away from a great man like Daryl?"

He was a great man. He was sweet, kind, gentle, generous, positive, smart, beautiful, and creative. He was far too good for me and he deserved so much better. I couldn't remember last night, but I was willing to bet every dollar I had that I was leaving for Daryl's own good. So he could find someone that would be able to give him everything his heart desired. I was just some homeless guy that he took pity on.

"He deserves better than me. It's better for him if I'm gone. He can find someone who will give him everything he wants and needs."

"He cares a lot about you, Dev. Whether you are here or not, it's still going to hurt him. He's already falling for you. That window of getting out clean without causing any pain has long since closed. You both fell hard and fast. It happens. That can be terrifying, but it can also be the best love you will ever experience in your life. That's not a love you let slip through your fingers. Especially over something like insecurities. You have a lot to offer someone, a lot to offer Daryl, but I can tell you right now, the only thing he wants from a partner is to be loved and respected. Now, that is something I know you would be able to give him."

I could hear a slight hurt undertone to his voice and I couldn't help but wonder if maybe he had lost a love like that himself. I knew better than to ask, though. Roland was more tight-lipped than a Royal Palace Guard.

"Life isn't that simple." It was a weak argument, but it was all I had right now. My head hurt too much to try and come back with something stronger and bulletproof.

"If it was, we would all be bored. I can call him, tell him you are here."

"No, don't. There wouldn't be a point. Once I can leave, I'm getting on that bus and he'll be free from me. It's what's best for him."

Roland patted the bed beside my arm as he got up. "Your body needs rest. I'll come by later to check in on you and sneak you in some food, if you're allowed."

My stomach turned at just the mere mention of hospital food. Nurses and doctors were always on your case to eat enough food so you could leave, but they never gave you anything you wanted to actually swallow.

Roland made his way to the door, but before he walked out of it he turned back to me one last time.

"A big part of respect is allowing your partner to make decisions for themselves. It's not up to you to decide if Daryl deserves better than you. That's on him to decide, and if you love him, you'll let him make that decision." And with that, he strode out the door.

He was right. I knew he was right and I hated it. Daryl did deserve to make the decision for himself, but I also knew it was one he would make based on emotions. He would pick me and that would only cause him pain later on in life. I was trying to avoid that for him, and for me.

A sharp pain shooting through my eyes told me I needed rest. I needed to get out of here and that was never going to happen if I didn't get some sleep to recover. Once I was able to leave, I would be getting on that bus and putting this town and Daryl in my rearview mirror. It was better for the both of us. I just hoped that Daryl would be able to forgive me one day.

CHAPTER ELEVEN

Daryl

WALKING INTO THE hospital was a terrifying experience.

The last time I was here was because Zane had been jumped. It had been terrifying then, too. At the time, we hadn't really been speaking all that much for a few years, but Zane had started making the effort. So when I walked in here after his attack, I was terrified that I would lose him before I ever truly got him back. Relief didn't even come close to what I felt when the doctor told us he would be okay.

I wanted to stay with him, but my parents had said we didn't need to sit there all night while he slept. By the time we got back in the morning, he was gone and my heart sank, fearing the worst. Only to find him outside of Jimmy's room and proclaiming his love for him.

When our father wanted him to deny it, I thought for sure he would. I thought he would give some lame excuse as to what he meant just to appease our father, only he surprised me again by being honest and strong. It was in that moment, I truly saw my big brother again and I couldn't have been more proud of him.

Now, here I was back at the hospital, and once again, someone I loved had been attacked and all but left for dead. If it hadn't been for Roland, Devon very well could have died. Roland had said he was pretty beat up, worse than what Zane had been, but that he would be okay in time. There were no permanent injuries and he was only beaten and nothing sexual happened to him. It was a relief to hear, but I knew it would have still brought up painful memories to my brother and Jimmy. Unlike their attackers, Devon's had been caught and would most likely face serious jail time for this crime.

"Remember, he's going to be fine. He's got a lot of bruises on him and his head and ribs are likely killing him. But he's going to be okay, and the Doc has him on some pain medication to help take the bulk of the pain away. He just needs rest," Roland advised us again and I could have sworn he was nervous.

I wasn't sure why Roland would be nervous about seeing Devon. He had already been by earlier to check in with him and stay with him until he woke up. The doctor hadn't allowed visitors until Devon was awake, but with Roland being a detective he could stay with him. It was something I greatly appreciated. I didn't want Devon waking up all alone and scared in a hospital bed.

"And he doesn't remember what happened?" Jimmy asked for clarification.

"Last thing he remembers is his shift

the night before. Doc said it was perfectly normal given the level of concussion he has. He may never remember the attack. Thankfully, we don't need him to. I was there at the end of it and the bus depot had cameras all along the outside. They got the whole thing. It's an open and shut case. Hopefully, with the bulk of the more dangerous members of the Draggos behind bars, other victims will come forward and finally press charges."

I could hear the slight hopefulness in his tone. He had been frustrated with victims not wanting to press charges because of the blowback that would be awaiting them. It was terrible, to be a victim but to be so afraid to press charges that they just lived with the injustice. They lived with knowing the one who hurt them was out there on the street, that they could easily see them walking by. For the sake of all those victims, and to prevent any future ones, I hoped they did come forward and band together to end the Draggos reign of terror, once and for all.

Roland led us down the hallway to Devon's hospital room. My heart pounded in my chest and I was fairly certain it was trying to escape. Either through my chest or up my throat. Despite knowing that Devon would be okay and nothing permanent was wrong with him.

I still found my hands trembling and my body flooded with fear. My mind was filled with endless "what if" possibilities. The most prominent, what if he took a turn for the worse and when we walked through those doors he wasn't there?

Could I handle losing someone that I loved?

I didn't even want to think about it, but my mind wouldn't stop going over the possibility that I could lose him before we had a chance at having something real. I wasn't kidding myself, either. I knew he was at the bus depot when he got attacked. He was leaving. Leaving me. But I refused to believe it was because he didn't care. The way he looked at me told me he cared. The sweet tender touches and moments that we shared told me he cared. Him leaving was not because he didn't care for me and I suspected it had a lot more to do with fear than the prospect of better work.

We had a lot we would need to talk

about and, hopefully, I would be able to get him to see that he didn't need to leave. That he could stay here and have a life with me, with our family. He wasn't alone anymore, and I knew it was going to take him some time to get used to that concept.

He had been struggling on his own since his brother died. First, it was with his father, and then on the streets. He didn't have to be strong and brave all the time. He could let himself feel and be vulnerable without the fear of being hurt, being hit. He had a lot of trauma he had to work through, but I was more than willing to work through it with him. He wasn't alone anymore and he needed to realize that.

"This is it. You ready?" Roland asked, keeping his gaze on me.

Letting out a slow, deep breath, I gave a nod.

Roland opened the door.

Walking into the room, my gaze immediately went to the bed, to Devon. He was awake, but he looked tired, as if he didn't get much sleep since Roland left. I could see the telltale signs of pain in his eyes and the crease on his forehead. Roland had warned us that he was covered in bruises, but hearing it and seeing it were two very different things. Seeing the state he was in, it instantly had tears building up in my eyes. The reality that I could have lost him last night was too fresh, too painful to even put into words.

"What are you doing here?" Devon's voice broke me out of my trance and I forced my body to move to the side of the bed.

"I'll give you guys some time," Roland said, before he purposefully strode out, closing the door behind him.

Zane and Jimmy moved around to the right side of Devon, but stayed back a bit, giving us some time.

"What are *we* doing here? You're in a hospital after getting attacked by six guys. Where else would we be?" I countered.

I wasn't expecting for him to be all open arms with us being here. He was in pain and I knew better than anyone when you weren't feeling great you just wanted to curl up and be alone. But the slight confusion and defensive tone to his voice had kind of pissed me off. It bothered me that he thought we wouldn't be here, that we wouldn't want to see him after what happened. Yes, we had only known each other less than a month, but that didn't change how I felt about him. It didn't change that we all lived together for three weeks. It didn't change that we were good people and would be worried about him, especially in his current state.

"Anywhere else. We've only known each other for three weeks, Daryl. It's not like I'm anyone important."

I could hear the sadness in his tone, even though he had tried to hide it. He wanted to be someone important to me. What he failed to realize was that he already was someone important. No, three weeks wasn't much time, especially in the grand scheme of things, but that didn't change how I felt.

It didn't change that I had been

falling for him almost from the moment he took my hand in the park. I was in love with him and I wasn't going to over-analyze that. Most would. Most would think it was impossible to love someone after such a short amount of time, but I wasn't most people. My brain and heart were wired differently and I could feel a deep love for someone if we made a strong connection.

Devon and I had made a strong connection. We made it that night we met and spent time together. You want to talk about love at first sight, this was it for me and I was not about to lose him now.

"Time is only a number. It doesn't matter if it has been three days or three years. When you feel a true connection with someone, time holds no meaning.

Yes, it's only been three weeks since you walked into my life, *our* lives, but it's been the best three weeks of my entire life."

"You're a part of the family now, Devon. I know you aren't used to having one, but you're just going to have to start getting used to it, because we aren't going anywhere," Jimmy added.

"It was hard at first for me, too. I was used to being on my own and not relying on anyone. But then Jimmy took a chance on me and it was the best thing to ever happen to me. I couldn't imagine ever going back to how I used to be. To being alone. You became a member of this family when Daryl brought you home that first night. Family, true family, doesn't give up on each other. No matter the struggles that one of us is going through. We're always there for each other, no matter what," Zane said with strength to his voice.

I couldn't have been more proud of Zane. He had worked hard to get used to opening up to people. To us. Jimmy had been his saving grace and I was so very thankful that he had been there for my brother when he needed him the most.

I snapped my gaze back over to Devon and I could see the emotions playing out in his eyes. This was all new to him and he wasn't handling it very well. He was clearly overwhelmed by the sheer emotions coming from all three of us. He obviously expected to remain alone in this world. He expected us to forget about him and move on with our lives. But I couldn't do that. None of us could. Whether he was here in town or not, we would all worry about where he was and if he was okay. He was so used to people hurting him, letting him down, not wanting him, that the concept of love and a family was completely foreign to him.

No more.

He deserved to know what love felt like.

He deserved to know what comfort and stability felt like.

I moved and sat down on the edge of the bed, being careful not to get too close and potentially cause him harm. "I know you went to that bus depot and I know you were planning on going to Baltimore. But I also know you care about me and I am willing to bet that scares you. That maybe you don't feel like you deserve to be with someone, or deserve to be cared for."

"You deserve better. You deserve better than me," he cut me off with a soft voice.

The fact that he thought he wasn't good enough for me was a load of crap. I didn't care that he'd been homeless. I didn't care if he was a dishwasher. I didn't care about any of it. All I cared about was how he made me feel. I cared about how he treated me and made me feel special and wanted. He was a kind, gentle, and sweet man.

Despite everything he had gone through, he still cared about people, still wanted to protect them and be a good man. He had every reason to throw in the towel and just give up, but he didn't. He continued to fight every day to keep people safe, to have a better life. He was a good man and I was lucky to have him in my life.

"That's bullshit. If you were going to leave because you didn't care about me, then I would have to accept that. But you don't get to decide what is best for me. You don't get to decide who is worthy and who isn't. I love you, and I don't care how crazy that sounds. I don't care that it's only been three weeks. I love you, Devon. It's my choice if I think you are worthy, and you are more than worthy of my love. You don't get to run away and take that choice from me. I know you care for me and I know you probably don't feel the same as I do, but—"

"Shut up," Devon snapped, and I could see the heat in his eyes, the fire. "You are a smart, beautiful, creative, kind, gentle, caring, and confident man. There isn't anything about you that I don't love. I love you, Daryl, and all I want is to be with you. If you'll still have me."

If I'll still have him?

Is he serious?

Of course I'd still have him. He's all I'd wanted. He's who I had been waiting for, and I couldn't imagine not having him in my life. Hearing that he loved me flooded my body with a warmth that I never wanted to get rid of.

I had dreamed of this moment. Of where we would finally say *I love you* to each other. I had pictured us out having a romantic dinner or watching the sunset at the park. I had never envisioned it would be in the hospital with Devon lying battered on the bed.

But it couldn't have been more perfect. The setting of which we said those three words didn't really matter. All that mattered was that we did finally say them to each other. We finally admitted it.

He loved me.

Just the thought brought a huge smile to my face.

"I love you, you idiot. Of course I want you."

Devon reached up with his left hand and wrapped it around the back of my neck and gently pulled me down. I was very careful to not put any weight against his chest as I gently pressed my lips to his. I made sure it stayed light, though, because he was injured and I didn't want to cause him any added pain. After a moment, we were forced to pull back when Jimmy's voice broke out into the quiet room.

"All right, you two. We don't need any alarms going off from lack of oxygen," he quipped.

I couldn't help the small chuckle at the images that brought forth. I could only picture how panicked the nurses would have been.

"We'll go grab some coffee and give you two a few minutes. Nothing crazy, though. We need him out of the hospital, not staying longer," Zane advised with a pointed look in my direction.

"What? I'll behave," I promised.

"Whatever you say, Squirt," Zane said with a playful wink before they both turned and left the room.

I shook my head and turned my attention back over to Devon, who was looking even more exhausted than when we came in.

"You sure you want more of them in your life?" I teased.

"I'm sure I want more of *you* in it," he responded with a smile that only caused my heart to flutter. "Come here, lay down with me."

"I don't want to hurt you," I said. I would have loved to lay down with him and provide him some comfort. But I also knew that broken ribs were no joke.

"You won't. My broken ribs are on my right side. Lay down with me."

I couldn't deny him that request, especially with knowing his ribs on his left were perfectly fine.

I kicked my shoes off before I got up and crawled under the covers. I made sure that none of my weight was on his chest, instead tucking myself into his left side.

Devon put his left arm around me and left his right on his stomach. I suspected it was the only comfortable position he could put his arm in. He placed a kiss on the top of my head as I spoke.

"You need sleep. I'll be here when you wake up, baby."

"I love you, Sweetheart."

"I love you, too."

I had no idea what the future would hold for the both of us after today. What I did know, though, was that I was really looking forward to experiencing it with the man that I loved.

CHAPTER TWELVE

Devon

Two Months Later

"YOU GOT EVERYTHING you need, Sweetheart?" I asked as I walked back into the bedroom I had been sharing with Daryl.

The past two months had been amazing and hard at the same time. Amazing, because I got to spend it with the man that I loved. Hard, because of my injuries that had just recently healed up. My ribs were still a bit tender if I turned the wrong way or if enough pressure was put on them. The doctor had said it was normal as they were just freshly healed. I still had some bruising on my ribs that was now an ugly yellow color.

Both Daryl and Zane had been terrific with me. Zane made sure I still able to work at the diner once I was healed up enough. Daryl had been overly cautious with me at first, terrified of hurting me further. It took a good week before I could finally get him to sleep in the bed with me again. It even took me until last week to convince him I was fine to have sex. Even then, he insisted on being on top, which was more than fine with me.

I never thought I would have this. A home with not only a man that I was madly in love with, but also brothers. Zane and Jimmy had taken me in when they didn't have to. They brought me into their family and welcomed me with open arms and no hesitation. I loved them both for that. I had finally found a family and I had zero interest in letting any of them go.

Hell, even Roland had become a member of my family, something I never would have expected. He was there every day I was in the hospital, always sneaking in food for me. It was the first time I had seen him outside of one of the soup kitchens and it turned out he was pretty amazing. He reminded me so much of Jay. Especially the fact that he had been in the Army for three years before he joined the police academy.

It was Roland who had shown me that my dream of helping people wasn't over. I couldn't be in the military without a spleen, but that didn't mean I couldn't help and protect the innocent people in this world. It was because of him that I applied to the Police Academy and had been accepted. I was set to start next month and I couldn't have been more excited. I was going to have a real future, a real career. I would be able to protect people, help those in town that were forgotten.

There was only one person I was missing. Tyler. I hadn't seen him since that night at the soup kitchen and I couldn't help but worry about him. I had been trying to find him so he could take over my job as a dishwasher. I knew he would be willing to do it, but I hadn't been able to find him. That didn't mean I would stop looking, though. I was going to find him again and I was going to make sure he was safe.

"I think so. If there's something I've forgotten then I can pick it up when I come back on the weekend," Daryl said, before he turned to me and I easily pulled him in for a hug. "This weekend only thing is going to suck."

"I know, but it's easier than you driving back and forth from Baltimore every day. That's too much strain on you, not to mention the gas money we'd need," I said flashing him a warm smile.

Daryl to let out a chuckle. "Might have to take out a loan with the gas prices right now. It's still going to suck and take a while to get used to."

"I know, Sweetheart, but we can video chat with each other every night and we'll see each other on weekends and holidays. A bit of space might not be so bad. Our relationship kind of went from zero to a hundred in no time flat."

Everything had gone very fast. I wasn't complaining, but I was worried that because we moved so fast and our emotions developed as quickly as they did, we would burn out. A flame could only burn so hot for so long and I didn't want us to lose what we had.

It was one of the reasons why I had agreed that it would be better for Daryl to stay on campus during the week. It would let us not only miss each other, but grow as individuals. Plus, I wanted him to have the fun experience of going to University. I wanted him to enjoy dorm parties and not having to worry about driving back home. This was an experience that I wanted him to have completely and not just part way.

It would be hard. There were going to be a lot of lonely nights and there would be arguments that happened in long-distance relationships, even if they were only Monday to Friday. It would challenge us, but I knew we were up for it and it would make us stronger in the end.

"I know and I agree it's important for us to grow as individuals as well as a couple. It's just going to be hard for the first couple of weeks. But I will have Jimmy there with me so if I am feeling homesick I can always go over to his place," Daryl said, flashing me a grin before he leaned up and pressed his warm lips to mine.

The feel of his lips against mine was something I was going to miss. Not being able to kiss him or touch him whenever I wanted to was going to be a hard reality. I was fully prepared to go through withdrawals, like a heroin addict.

All too soon, Daryl pulled back and I knew he needed to head out. He was driving up with Jimmy and if they didn't leave soon they would hit the heavy traffic. The drive would be hard enough, they didn't need to be stuck in a traffic jam as well.

I picked up his last bag before we made our way out of the apartment and down to the awaiting car. Daryl went over to give Zane a hug as I put his bag into the trunk and closed it.

"I'll keep an eye on him," Jimmy said

with a wink, and it had me opening my arms to the very sweet man.

Jimmy easily welcomed the hug and I knew he would keep Daryl safe and sane while he adjusted to being in Baltimore and in school. I wasn't worried, though. Daryl would make friends in minutes and he was so talented with creating video games. He was going to take that school by storm and he would become a famous video game designer one day. I couldn't have been more proud of him. Pulling back, we both made our way over to our respective man.

"This isn't goodbye, it's an I'll see you later. Remember that," I said as I wrapped my arms around Daryl's hips.

"I know. Still sucks, but I know. I left you a little surprise on your laptop for later on tonight. Just make sure you watch it alone and with headphones," Daryl said with a playful smirk. I couldn't help but groan at what could be awaiting me.

My need to feel his lips against my own one last time was too great. I needed to taste him once more before I had to go all week without him. Daryl melted at my touch and I had to remind myself that we were in the middle of the street with his big brother right there. If we had been in our room, he would already be naked and underneath me.

I forced every ounce of love that I had into the kiss. Focusing my mind on memorizing the smallest details of his lips and the way they felt against my own. It might only be a week, but to me it was going to feel like an eternity before I could kiss him again. If I had to wait that long, I was going to make sure it was a kiss that the both of us would not soon forget.

"I remember when you used to try and kiss my very soul out of me."

Jimmy's voice broke the spell between us. Both of us sent Zane and Jimmy a well deserved glare for their rude interruption. It only caused them both to laugh.

"Relax, it gets easier," Zane offered, but it was of little comfort to me at that moment.

"Come on, we need get on the road if we are going to stand a chance at eating dinner tonight," Jimmy said, giving Zane one last quick peck on the lips before heading for the car.

With a final squeeze, I had no choice but to allow Daryl to join Jimmy. Zane moved over to stand beside me and placed a comforting hand on my shoulder. It was nice, but it wasn't his touch I craved. Together, we stood there, smiling and waving goodbye as the men we loved drove off.

"It really does get easier and it will make the time that you do get to share together more special," Zane offered.

He was right. I knew he was, but that didn't make this hurt any less. Two months ago, I was fully prepared to leave all of this behind. Leave Daryl behind. I was dead set on putting it all in my rearview mirror. I never expected to be the one slowly disappearing in his rearview. At least I could be thankful that he was only going to school and we hadn't broken up.

Looking back now, I could completely

say that getting on that bus would have been the worst decision of my life. In a way, I was glad that Luis and his thugs had jumped me. I would gladly go through all of that pain a million times over if it meant I would have not only Daryl in my life, but the lovely family that I have now as well. I had gone from the homeless man that had nobody, to the man who had not only a home and a family, but a bright future with the world's most amazing man.

For quite possibly the first time in my life, I could honestly say I was excited for what the future had in store for me. I just knew it was going to be a bright one with Daryl by my side.

Thank you for reading.

Watch for Jaded, From The Edge,
Book Three, at your favorite online
retailer.

Turn the page for a preview!

PREVIEW

Roland

*"YOU KNEW WHAT you signed up for!"
The strength of my voice made the words
echo off of our kitchen walls.*

*"I didn't sign up for this! I didn't sign
up for a military life!"*

*"You knew I was in the military when
we met, Shane. This isn't some new
thing. I told you I wanted to be a Ranger*

and in order for that to happen I have to move to Georgia. Why can't you be supportive?"

"Supportive? Supportive of you going out on dangerous missions. Supportive of you getting injured or killed? How the hell am I supposed to be supportive of that? I've entertained you being in the military and humored you, because I thought it was a phase. I thought you would come to your senses and see that a life behind a desk was better for us. How the hell are we supposed to get married and have a real life together if you can't even admit that you're gay?"

"It's not that simple. You know that I can't just come out to the guys. If they have a problem with it, they might not have my back in the field. You said you didn't care. That it didn't bother you."

"And you actually thought I would be happy to live a life hidden in the shadows forever? That I would be happy to hear the man who supposedly loves me talking about whatever imaginary girl he banged just so the guys will feel more comfortable? You promised me marriage, you promised me kids, and now you have taken all of that away. I won't be your dirty secret!"

"You're not, but you can't keep pressuring me like this. It's my life and I'll live it how I see fit!"

"Then it's a life you'll be living without me. I'm not going to be kept hidden away, and I'm not going to be left here while you are out there, never knowing if you're coming home to me." Shane grabbed his car keys and stormed toward the door.

"Fine, if that's how you feel I don't

need you. You can get the hell out of my life!"

The house shook as the front door slammed shut.

My breath caught in my throat as I shot up in bed. My body was damp from the sweat that covered it and I could feel the tremble that threatened to overtake my whole body. This was not my first nightmare. Hell, this wasn't even the thousandth. They often plagued me and I was never lucky enough to wake up not remembering them. If it wasn't my time overseas from the war that I fought for three years, it was of my own personal hell. The night that changed everything in my life. The night I lost the most amazing man. A man that could very well have been my soulmate.

And it was all my fault.

My own stupidity that drove him away that night.

When you are twenty-one everything in life seems so simple. I was so stupid back then, so naive to believe that I could have a military life and be gay without it ever affecting my job or my home life. I thought the best solution was to hide it, like it was some disease that I needed to keep secret.

Stupid.

So unbelievably stupid.

A quick look at the clock showed me it was just after four in the morning and I knew I wouldn't be able to get back to sleep. Letting out a sigh, I forced my sore and tired body to move. After eleven years, I had become used to functioning off little to no sleep. Being in the army for three years had started the normalcy of little sleep between boot camp, training, and missions. Then my time as a New York cop solidified it. When you work as a homicide detective in a big city like New York, you get used to getting called out of bed at any hour of the evening and working two or three days straight with only bad station house coffee to keep you going.

Making my way into the bathroom, I did my best to avoid the mirror. I knew what would be looking back at me. A man with red, tired eyes that carried a haunted look in them. For the most part, I could cover up my pain, push through it and wear a mask during the day. People in this small town didn't know anything personal about me and that was how I wanted it to be.

I had only been here for four years,

when the toll of being a homicide detective became too much. I was handling it just fine, but then the Michelle Wilson case came my way and I realized that I couldn't do it anymore.

Michelle Wilson was a beautiful four year old little girl who had been found dead in a dumpster four years ago. It wasn't just because of her age, it was because she had been raped and tortured thirty-six hours before her death.

She was never reported missing.

The investigation took me three weeks to solve. Three weeks of having to re-read the Coroner's report. Three weeks of having to see the photos of the brutal acts done to her. Three weeks of interviewing her parents who were completely devastated.

Three weeks for me to discover that her so-called devastated parents were actually her kidnappers.

Michelle Wilson's prints and DNA finally came back from the lab and they matched a missing two year old girl named Rebecca Watts. She had been kidnapped one night while the parents were away at dinner. She had been left with a babysitter who was killed trying to protect her. Rebecca Watts was one of thirty-six children that had been kidnapped for a child sex trafficking ring. Her death had broken the case wide open and with the help of the Feds, we were able to shut it down.

The case itself wasn't necessarily the part that broke me. It was afterward, when the whole precinct was celebrating the win. To them it was a win, but to me it was a great loss.

Because we had failed Rebecca.

We had failed her parents and now they would forever be haunted by her death and what she had experienced in the last two years of her life. We had saved only ten out of the thirty-six that we knew to be out there. The other twenty-six were already sold and gone. We had lost them.

There was no win.

There was nothing to celebrate.

It was in that moment that I realized I couldn't do it anymore. So, when I saw the posting for a new detective here, I immediately applied, and given my experience in a large city, I was hired on the spot.

Now, three years later, I was trying to do what I could to keep this small town safe. There weren't really murders that happened here, but there were crimes, nonetheless. There were three gangs that ran the criminal enterprises in town, two of which were small-time and nothing to worry about too much.

Drugs were in every town and we did our best to make sure we didn't have any labs cooking them. The Draggos were the ones that caused the most violence and harm in the town. We had been working on trying to get them shut down, but with no victims willing to come forward, it had put a serious delay in the process.

At least, until six of their top guys made the mistake in attacking Devon St. James at the bus depot two months back. The whole thing was caught on video surveillance and even if it hadn't been, I knew Devon would have testified against them.

He had been homeless since he was seventeen, but the man always made sure to help people and keep the streets safe. The whole reason the Draggos had targeted him was because he attacked their leader as he was trying to rape a young girl in an alley close to eight months ago. For the past two months, we had finally been able to start taking down the Draggos, and soon enough, we would have them all locked up.

After relieving myself, I headed back into my bedroom to change my sweat-soaked pants, something that was almost a daily task. I changed into some clean, dry sweat pants and a hoodie before I threw on my running shoes and hit the pavement.

Running had never been something I was interested in, until my boot camp days. I had discovered that it was a great way for me to get my spinning thoughts in order. Whenever I felt like I needed a moment to breathe, I would go for a run and it helped me to feel better. It helped to calm my racing mind and allow me to think clearly.

I wished I had just gone for a run that night with Shane.

Maybe everything would have turned out differently if I had.

Forcing that painful thought aside, I coaxed my mind to think about things that I could control.

Like Tyler.

He was relatively new to one of the soup kitchens that I volunteer at. That same soup kitchen was where I met

Devon for the first time, and now he had become a member of my family.

Tyler was different compared to the other homeless people I'd interacted with. To begin with, he was young. If I had to guess, he was fifteen at most. He should have been in a home and not sleeping on the streets.

I had often tried to talk with him, but he was very shy. He never looked me in the eye and whenever I was around he seemed to shrink into himself.

I was used to that reaction, though, just because of my size. I did workout. I had always been a gym guy. Even when I was sixteen I would often work out whenever I got the chance. I still do it a few days a week to keep my body in good shape. The result, though, is that I was very buff and with that, intimidation always followed. Between being in the army and in the police force, my love for working out only deepened. It came in handy when I needed to intimidate a suspect, but it also meant it took victims a few minutes to get comfortable with me.

Living in a smaller town like this, I didn't have to worry too much about the victims. Everyone knew everyone, essentially, and people here all knew that despite my size I was like a teddy bear. If I could protect you, then I would. I would lay down my life for anyone in this town.

I was worried about Tyler, though, and I suspected there had been abuse in his life just by the way he reacted to me. He was afraid of me and I could tell. Anyone that saw us together could tell. I hated that he was afraid of me. I would never hurt him, but it was going to take time before he understood that. Before he truly one hundred percent believed that he was safe around me. It was going to take time, but I was never afraid of hard work.

My worry for Tyler had increased some over the past two months, though. I hadn't seen him at the soup kitchen and neither had Devon. I knew he had a car. How he was driving it without a license, I didn't know, but he could have easily driven off to another town.

I was hoping he hadn't left town. I would have loved to help him try and get back on his feet. Try and find a safe place for him to live. We didn't have many foster homes, but we did have some. It was why I reached out to my friend, Isaiah, in Child Protective Services. I need to know more of his story, but I also needed to know what foster home he was in hiding from so he could be put into a safe one.

What most people didn't understand about the homeless community here in town, was that they weren't all alcoholics or drug addicts. The majority of them had some type of mental illness that had been either undiagnosed, or untreated. Some were even runaways, like Devon, who had to escape an abusive situation and just could never get back on their feet.

Thankfully, Devon had managed to get back on his feet with the help of Daryl and his older brother, Zane. Devon was now going to be in the Police Academy, and I knew he was going to make one hell of a cop. I was looking forward to working with him and mentoring him.

Devon was safe and now it was time to make sure Tyler was. He was one of the few that I could help and I was not about to let him slip through my fingers.

***

"All right, I've gotten the bulk of the dishes cleaned up, Martha," I said as I dried my hands off.

It was just after seven and the mass of the dinner rush had finished. I had volunteered at St. Marks Soup Kitchen for close to three years now. I often volunteered my time for various charities in town. I wanted to make sure the community and the people in it knew that they could trust me.

That I was a friendly face whenever they needed it.

I knew that people in a small town didn't hate the police as much as they seemed to in a major city like New York, but I wasn't going to kid myself into believing that everyone loved the police in town, either. Small town or not, that didn't mean people weren't judgmental or corrupt.

In fact, I often found from my dealings with other local law enforcement agencies around New York City, that those small towns had all sorts of corruption within them. To some, it might not make much sense, but to me it did.

Who better to be corrupt than the mayor of a small town?

It wasn't like anyone would notice or

suspect anything.

After all, what small town had corruption in it?

It was that novice assumption that made it possible for bad people to hurt a lot of innocent people, even if it was their pocketbook they were targeting.

"Thank you, Roland. You are so much help around here. I honestly don't know what I would do without you." Martha placed a kiss on my cheek and it warmed my heart.

Martha was the sweetest seventy-two year old you could ever meet. She was also the most fierce seventy-two year old I had ever met. She wasn't your typical grandmother. She ran ten miles three times a week, and she kept a bat next to her bed in case anyone was stupid enough to break into her house.

If you walked into her house, you would think you walked into a time warp. It was the perfect cookie cutter home from back in the fifties, right down to the ugly brown shag carpet. She kept it pristine and there was even plastic on the furniture.

She was one of a kind and she ran the show here. There were only two soup kitchens in town, there should have been more, but the officials believed two was more than enough, just like one shelter was more than enough. It wasn't enough, nowhere near it, but there was no money to be made helping the homeless. It was a sad fact, but it was a fact, nonetheless. The town was trying to grow.

I had been getting crap from my Captain about trying to get better control on the homeless community. Trying to get them pushed back into the shadows for when the developers come into town. Mayor Jenson was trying to win his reelection and apparently the way he was going about it was to make sure the town grew.

I wasn't against growth, but small towns survived off the mom and pop businesses that make up the town. They survived because of tourists wanting to come and see the quaint town. I wasn't sure how well it would go over to have large construction sites all over town, but it was something we would all have to deal with soon enough.

"Why don't you head home and I'll handle the closing tonight. I can see that your hip has been bothering you tonight."

"That's very sweet of you, but I can't leave you here all alone to handle closing."

"It's not very busy tonight, there's only a few people hanging around. Go home, put your feet up, and watch your soap," I said, flashing her a warm smile.

She would cave.

I knew she would.

She loved her soap operas and she made sure to record them every day. I had even shown her how to use the DVR that she had gotten from her kids for Christmas. Once she knew how to use it, there was no stopping her. She was a recording queen with over two hundred hours of recordings to go through.

"Oh, all right. If you're sure."

"I am. Go on and get out of here," I said, flashing her a big smile.

She gave me a grin in return and then she headed off to grab her coat and purse.

I made my way back out to the front and started to put together the last few plates that I could store in the fridge for tomorrow. Normally around eight, the place got quiet and I would close up. The sole shelter in town tended to fill up quickly, so everyone who needed a place to stay the night would flock there in the hope of getting a bed.

It could be very busy here when there was a storm. Once the shelters filled up, anyone who didn't get a bed would seek sanctuary here for as long as they could. When I had been left to close up on those nights, I would try and hold off for as long as possible, especially if the weather was horrible. I hated knowing that I would have to kick people out who had nowhere to go, nowhere safe to be. I had been trying to fight with the town council about getting more shelters built so the homeless would have a safe place to be at night, but so far there was no budging them.

At the sound of footsteps, I turned to face whoever had approached the serving station. To my surprise, it was Tyler. I had been trying to find him for two months and when I finally saw him again, he had found me.

He also found me while he sported a nasty black eye. Seeing it sent a wave of anger throughout my body. He was just a kid. He didn't deserve to be hit.

"Who the fuck hit you?"

RUNAWAY

Watch for Jaded at your favorite online retailer.

If you enjoyed Runaway, the second book in the From The Edge series, please return to your retailer and leave a review. Even a few words can mean the world to an author. Plus it helps other readers like you find our work too.
Share the love! ;)

OTHER BOOKS BY EVIE

Federal Protection Agency

Mason
Rafe
Ryzen
Cooper
Noah
Damien
Sebastian
Gabe
Logan

Ruthless Empire

Courting Danger
Chasing Danger
Kissing Danger

Smokejumpers

Hawke
Cyrus
Jase
Gage
Jackson
Xavier

Jasper Springs
Cade
Dawson
Drew
Grayson
Riley
Mitch

From The Edge
Shattered
Runaway
Jaded
Rescue
Hidden
Tormented

Gray Vale Pack
His Fated Mate
His Wounded Warrior
His Healing Heart

ABOUT THE AUTHOR

Evie Riley is a prolific, neurodivergent author known for her captivating MM romance novels. She has gained a significant following and topped the LGBT+ action and adventure bestseller charts with her series.

Evie's writing style often explores dark and gritty themes where her men must overcome difficult obstacles in their search for love, but she has also ventured into sweeter small-town romances, incorporating tropes like enemies-to-lovers, friends-to-lovers, age-gap, and forced proximity. She is known for crafting engaging romantic suspense novels and has a knack for creating interconnected series worlds that keep readers invested.

EVIE RILEY

Interestingly, Ms. Riley has hinted at exploring new genres, such as Alien Omegaverse Romance, in the future.

Outside of writing, she enjoys spending time at the beach and has a quirky personality, described by her partner as ranging from cute to deadly, depending on her blood-chocolate levels.

Evie spends her nights writing bad boys in love, and her days wrangling the sweet boys she loves.

www.ingramcontent.com/pod-product-compliance
Lightning Source LLC
Chambersburg PA
CBHW071407200726
48294CB00002B/306